"Good evening, princess."

She went very still. This was no fantasy. He was in her room—dark and seductive—and he'd gotten past the locks on her door!

She whirled and leapt to her feet. "What are you doing here?"

"This is our wedding night." André strolled lazily into the room. "I thought we should spend at least some of it together."

"No. That wasn't our agreement." She began backing away.

"Just a toast, my dear. To seal our bargain."

But that wasn't all he had on his mind. Not by a long shot. His eyes were a little too dark, his gaze all too blatantly filled with masculine approval as he perused her scantily clad body. Her skin flushed and she folded her arms across her waist.

"Look, André, this has been a rather stressful day. I'd like to call it quits and go to bed. Alone," she added pointedly.

He cocked an eyebrow, boldly glancing over at the huge bed. "Pity," he murmured as the champagne cork popped.

Dear Reader,

American Romance is "Goin' to the Chapel" with three soon-to-be-wed couples. Only thing is, saying "I do" is the furthest thing from their minds!

So glad you could join us for the second wedding in this trilogy of veils and vows.

As a child, Charlotte Maclay was told she was distantly related to the Queen of Sweden. Since she hasn't been called to service yet, she let her characters have the fun of living out that fantasy in *The Kidnapped Bride*.

Hope you're enjoying walking down the aisle with us!

Regards,

Debra Matteucci
Senior Editor & Editorial Coordinator
Harlequin Books
300 E. 42nd St.
New York, NY 10017

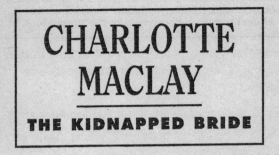

CHARLOTTE MACLAY

THE KIDNAPPED BRIDE

Harlequin Books

TORONTO • NEW YORK • LONDON
AMSTERDAM • PARIS • SYDNEY • HAMBURG
STOCKHOLM • ATHENS • TOKYO • MILAN
MADRID • WARSAW • BUDAPEST • AUCKLAND

ISBN 0-373-16537-4

THE KIDNAPPED BRIDE

Chapter One

The customs official held his rubber stamp above her passport, studying Nicole LeDeaux as though she were some kind of rodent trying to sneak into his country. "Reason for your visit?" he asked in the curt manner of bureaucrats who relish their authority.

"I'm here to buy antiques." She resented anyone looking down his nose at her, and was exhausted by her ten-hour flight from the States, hardly able to stand, much less think coherently. "Of course," she said, her fatigue making her reckless, "I've been told I'm related to the last reigning king of Margolis. If I find the time, I thought I'd drop by the castle and pick up my inheritance."

The customs officer's lips drew into a grim line and his eyes narrowed as he scrutinized her so closely she felt heat creep up her neck. "You must not joke about such things, *mademoiselle*."

"Who's joking?" Besides, she doubted the man had laughed even once in the past ten years. At least not while he was on the job.

"Your words are very dangerous. There are factions in this country—"

"Look, I'm tired. I need a bath, a decent meal that doesn't come in plastic wrap, and a good night's sleep. Will you please stamp my passport and let me get to my hotel?"

The rubber stamp slammed onto the open page of her passport, leaving a purple smudge. "As you wish, *mademoiselle*. But remember, you were warned."

So much for her welcome to Margolis, she thought as she grabbed the handle to her suitcase and tugged; her own fault, she admitted. She'd never told anyone that silly story passed down by her grandmother, at least not since she'd been a kid.

Related to the king of Margolis? Utter nonsense.

"THERE SHE IS—coming out of the hotel now. The woman who arrived at the airport last night."

From his vantage point across the street at an outdoor café, André Montiard studied the woman they had been waiting for. Her long auburn hair was pulled back from her face and she wore tinted glasses against the bright morning sun that flooded the public square. Walking with the easy stride he'd learned to recognize as American, she made her way toward the cathedral, a typical first stop for every tourist. Her skirt swung across her hips and shifted gracefully at her knees, revealing well-shaped calves.

"Nice legs," he commented to his friend Sebastian.

"You need to worry about more than her legs, my friend. Word has spread very fast about her arrival in San Margo. If she is the sole heir to the throne—"

"*If* is a big word."

"—then you can be sure Hendrik Meier-Wahl will be out looking for her, too. He'd love to get his hands on every jewel in the crown if he could."

"I'm sure he would. He has his greedy little fingers in every other pie in this country."

"His reelection might well be assured if he had the ear of a queen."

André dragged his gaze away from the very pleasant sight of Nicole LeDeaux's swaying hips to look at his friend. "Our country is no longer ruled by a monarchy, or has that small detail escaped your notice?" he asked dryly.

"The people have long memories. There is always some fascination with royalty. Nostalgia, at the very least. They might even think this woman, if we were to restore the monarchy, would be a tourist attraction like the British queen is. You know, strutting around on a horse in front of her personal bodyguards, cutting ribbons at openings..."

Unconcerned with his friend's comments, André stretched out his long legs and crossed his ankles, studying the spotless shine on his Italian loafers. "What this country needs is more industry, not pomp and circumstance. Certainly not more taxes to support a useless royal family."

"Then I suggest you take some immediate action before Hendrik beats you to the punch, as the Americans might say."

"Such as?"

"Courtship would be a good beginning. If that fails…" Sebastian shrugged his narrow shoulders in a thoroughly European way. "I recommend kidnapping and marrying her."

André choked on his coffee, and his burst of laughter drew stares from the customers at neighboring tables. What a ludicrous idea. Sebastian had outdone himself this time. Granted, as they'd grown up together on the Montiard estates, Sebastian had always come up with some crazy plan that had gotten them both into mischief…and had often gotten them caned. But this notion topped them all.

When he could pull himself together, André combed his fingers through his hair and addressed Sebastian. "I've probably had a dozen women propose to *me* in the last year. Somehow I doubt I'll ever have to kidnap a woman in order to convince her to marry me." Of course, each of the women who had expressed an interest in matrimony had really been after a large chunk of his bank account. None had made any pretense of learning about the man who held title to all of that wealth. A genetic shortcoming of all women, he gathered, based on the same sort of experience his father had endured.

"If you say so. But word has already spread that is exactly Hendrik's plan."

"Are you serious?" The thought stunned André. "The man is sixty years old and ugly as sin. It would take more than a kidnapping to convince any woman in her right mind to marry him."

"Not if he took her to his hunting lodge," Sebastian suggested, "drugged her and kept her there until she agreed. Afterward . . . no one would pay heed to her story if Hendrik still ran the show."

André hadn't considered that possibility. Nor would he put it past Hendrik if such a plan fit in with his schemes. The man had no conscience. The only reason he had survived so long as prime minister of Margolis was that he kept half the thieves and crooks in the country employed as government officials. In turn, they strong-armed any poor soul who objected. It was a system of machine politics André had vowed to stop the day his older brother had met with a fatal accident.

"Of course," Sebastian said in lazy challenge, "if you fear your actions might upset Marlene, then by all means, we will have to find some other solution to the problem."

"What might or might not disturb my late brother's sister-in-law is of little concern to me. Long ago I made it clear she and I had no future together." Indeed, as a young man André had struggled to make Marlene accept his lack of interest without damaging her fragile ego. Not an easy task in the face of such a determined, possessive female.

"Naturally, you made your feelings clear."

"I admit she was not a good loser. But she has recovered from whatever small inconvenience I caused her, I am sure."

"Most certainly."

André glanced up to see the LeDeaux woman standing on the steps of the cathedral looking around the square. A few hours spent in courtship would not be an onerous task, he concluded. Her figure, at least, was worthy of further exploration. Whether or not she could meet his connoisseur tastes had yet to be determined.

He smiled to himself. Fortunately he had no pressing business matters for the rest of the day.

Spotting an old flower vendor making her way through the café hawking her wares, he signaled to her. With a few Margolis francs he purchased a handful of violets. A small bouquet ought to provide a reasonable introduction for an impressionable young American tourist.

Rising from his chair, he tossed another few coins onto the table, and said, "The least I can do is welcome the young lady to our country." His eyes met Sebastian's and they exchanged a knowing look.

"I thought perhaps you would be interested." Sebastian touched three fingers to his lips and tossed a kiss in the air. "Good luck, my friend."

"Talent, skill and experience are far more important than luck. Even when a man sets off to seduce a princess."

Laughing at their shared joke, André strolled toward the cathedral. He had always enjoyed American women. They were a fascinating combination of naïveté and sophistication that made for quite a challenge.

Before he had gone far, he noticed a black Citroën cruising slowly through the square, headed, as he was, toward the cathedral. A government car, he would have recognized it anywhere. He quickened his pace when he spotted one of Hendrik's henchmen behind the wheel and another in the passenger seat.

"Damn," he muttered under his breath. Sebastian's sources were rarely wrong. The LeDeaux woman was about to be in serious trouble and so was André's country. As a matter of pride, he couldn't let that happen.

He broke into a sprint.

NICOLE WALKED slowly down the steps. She had a dozen antique stores to visit and wanted to travel through the countryside to see what she could pick up in the way of good buys at local flea markets. But she was reluctant to rush. She simply wanted to absorb for a few more minutes the romantic European ambience of San Margo before she got down to serious business. Louis XIV chairs and Spode china could wait awhile. One of the reasons she'd saved and scrimped in the hope of opening her own shop was to have these annual opportunities to travel. No sense wasting a single moment of this, her first trip abroad.

Granted, Margolis had been a nostalgic choice for starting her adventure. No doubt a result of her grandmother's fanciful stories, which Nicole made a point to *not* take seriously.

She waited at the curb as a car approached, its wheels frightening pigeons into the air. Her gaze followed the flight of the birds as they circled upward, spiraling toward the dramatic spires of the cathedral. She smiled. A picture-perfect kingdom. For a moment she could almost imagine being queen in this lovely setting. Pity her ancestors had emigrated to America.

The car halted and the door opened in front of her. A big, brawny man, who somehow looked out of place dressed in a pin-striped suit, started to get out of the vehicle. His pock-marked face sported a crooked nose that must have collided one too many times with an immovable object.

She stepped back out of his way, her head turning as she heard the sound of running feet coming from the opposite direction.

An instant later, a man wearing a black turtleneck sweater and equally dark pants grabbed Nicole by the hand and dragged her away from the cathedral.

"Help!" she screamed, panic threatening.

"Don't be afraid, Princess," he assured her as he pulled her into a narrow alley between two red-brick buildings. "I'm not going to hurt you."

"What are you doing?" she cried. He was tall and lean, and as agile as an athlete.

"Saving you from Hendrik. You'll thank me later, I assure you."

The brute in the car? she wondered, confusion muddling her thinking.

Her sandals slipped on a patch of wet cobblestones as they rounded a corner, and the man steadied her, his hands surprisingly gentle for a guy who was literally dragging her down the street. "Who's Hendrik?" she asked.

"A toad. With big, popping eyes. He'd eat you alive, Princess." He kept on going, with her in tow.

"Stop!" She dug in her sandaled heels as best she could. "You're yanking my arm out of its socket."

He turned into another alley, then pulled her into an alcove, a doorway maybe, she wasn't quite sure. She did know she was breathing hard and he was pressing his body protectively against hers, making her incredibly aware of the ribbed flatness of his belly, the breadth of his chest, and an erotic, leathery scent that had to be his after-shave. Appreciation warred with her good sense.

"Please, will you tell me what's going on?"

"You were about to be kidnapped."

Right. As if that weren't exactly what was happening to her now. Though this fellow was certainly better looking than the man in the car. "You must be imagining things. Why would anyone want to kidnap me?" This guy included.

"You are heir to the Margolis throne, are you not?"

She felt the blood drain from her face. The damn customs man! "That's just an old story—"

"A great many people believe it is true." He cupped her face with his hand, lifting her chin. She gazed into eyes the color of coal, as dark as liquid smoke, with a surprising hint of tenderness lurking in their depths. "It's a very dangerous story." His voice was low and raspy, strangely intimate.

A shiver of anxiety sped down her spine. "I'm an antique dealer. That's all." At least, she would be once she'd made her first buys and opened the store she'd leased.

He quirked her a half smile, curling lips that were so totally sensuous they looked designed to drag kiss after moist kiss from a woman's mouth. "You are far more than that, my dear," he said softly. He gave her a long, hot look from the top of her head down to her toes, effectively undressing her.

She bristled at his cavalier attitude, all the while aware of a tight, forbidden thrill racing through her veins. She never, *ever* reacted to a man like this, much less to a stranger; it simply wasn't her style.

She braced her hands on his unyielding chest. "I think I'd like to go back to my hotel now."

Someone shouted nearby and there was the renewed sound of running feet.

He rolled his eyes, muttering what she took to be a curse under his breath. "Time to implement Plan B."

"What's that?" Her voice hitched.

"Later, Princess." Grabbing her hand again, he pulled her out of the alcove and they raced down the alley, dodging brimming trash bins and weaving their way through a labyrinth of ancient streets so narrow and winding Nicole knew she'd never find her way back to the main square again. Wrought-iron balconies on either side nearly touched above her, blocking out any possibility of sunlight reaching the damp cobblestones. The scent of rotting garbage along with the smell of cooked cabbage assailed her senses.

He found a tiny doorway at the back of a stone building and shoved their way inside.

It was dark, musty, and smelled of candle wax.

Her heart thundering, Nicole gasped for breath. They were in a church, she realized, a small sanctuary she dearly hoped would provide her safe haven from this wild man who had dragged her through the streets and alleys of San Margo.

"Father," he called to the priest kneeling at the railing.

The old man looked up. His face broke into a broad smile and he levered his rotund body to a standing position. "André, my son. We have missed seeing you at mass these last few—"

"I know, Father."

"Your immortal soul is in grave—"

"Not now, Father. I need a favor."

"Of course, my son. Whatever you ask, God will—"

"I want you to marry us. Now."

Nicole gasped.

The priest's smile vanished. "These matters should not be rushed."

"There will be a large contribution for your parish," André promised. "Tomorrow."

"Don't listen to him," Nicole pleaded. "I don't even know—"

"Tomorrow?" the priest questioned. His vestments looked old and worn. "How much?"

"The House of Montiard owes you a great deal, Father. We have been lax in our support of late. Name your price."

The old man smiled.

"Wait!"

"Now, Padre! Say the words you need to and we'll be gone. You can fill out the forms later."

The priest began mumbling words so fast Nicole couldn't understand them. The man called André shoved a tiny bouquet of violets into her hands. A bridal bouquet? she wondered frantically. She clasped them tightly because she simply didn't know what else to do even as she was trying to tell the priest she wasn't the least bit interested in marrying a total stranger, in a foreign land, and she'd call the nearest consulate at the first chance she got. But nobody listened.

"Say 'I will,' Nicole," André ordered.

"I will—" The word "not" was swallowed as he covered her mouth with his in a deep, probing kiss. Her body pulsated with the electrifying power of his touch. This wasn't happening, or so her rational mind told her. Her body responded in a far different way however. Hot. Needy. She leaned wantonly into his kiss as sensations swirled around her, within her, curling like fiery lava through her veins.

She moaned into his mouth and heard a surprised response, low and throaty, and almost as needy as hers.

He broke the kiss, his fingers pressing into her upper arms. She stood unsteadily on her wobbly legs, looking into eyes that had grown even darker with his arousal. His lips glistened with moisture from their kiss and his breath swept her face in a heated caress. Slowly, he drew the back of one finger along her cheek. Goose bumps tracked a path down her spine.

"As long as our marriage lasts, may it be a pleasure for both of us." He drew his thumb slowly across her lower lip.

Helplessly, she shook her head. "You're crazy."

"Probably."

Again there were noises outside, angry sounds, and a door opened, sending a streak of sunlight into the dim corners of the church. The silhouette of a very large man appeared in the doorway.

"Come on," André ordered. "We must leave."

"I'm not—" Her throat caught on a combination of excitement and terror. "I'm not going anywhere with you."

"Ah, Princess. I wish there were time to explain."

With that, he picked her up and slung her over his shoulder as though she were nothing more than a roll of carpeting.

She screamed. . . .

Chapter Two

She was still screaming five miles out of town.

André's sleek Ferrari convertible whipped along a road so narrow and winding it appeared to have been engineered with all of the skill of a wandering cow. Wild berry bushes draped themselves over low rock walls bordering the road right up to the asphalt, so close there was no room for a car to pull off except for the occasional entrance to some farm.

Nicole's hair snapped across her face. She dragged the flyaway strands from her mouth, then closed it. Her voice had grown hoarse, and by now there was no one to hear her screams, anyway. Those in town who had noticed her frantic efforts to attract attention had mostly waved to André, their smiles amused, as though the guy kidnapped women every day of the week. And maybe he did. He certainly seemed at ease with the situation.

Nicole was not.

"Please, Mr. Montiard, if that's your name—André—just stop a minute and let me out of the car. I'll walk back to town. It's not all that far, and I promise I won't say a word to anyone about what's happened." He could count on her being on the next plane out of the country before anyone could say Rumpelstiltskin. He could even keep the puddle of violets she'd tossed to the floorboard.

He shot her a rakish grin, a smile that creased both his cheeks in a thoroughly endearing way. In another time and place, she would have found his dark good looks attractive. But not when she was angry enough to spit tacks.

"Now why would I want to leave my pretty new bride way out here in the middle of nowhere?"

"I am *not* your bride. I never said yes to anything. There's got to be a law in this country against kidnapping. The U.N. has sanctions against white slavery, you know."

He didn't stop smiling, which infuriated her even more. "I'll pay you," she offered. "I'll sign over my traveler's checks. My credit card. Whatever you want." Even a pint of blood, if that's what it took.

"I assure you, my dear Nicole, I neither want nor need your money. My methods may seem a bit unorthodox at the moment, but I have only your best interests at heart. No harm will come to you as long as you are under my protection. So, please, enjoy the countryside." He made a casual sweep with his hand that took in the rural scenery—rows of trees weighed

down with ripening fruit, wide expanses of hay in
open fields, picturesque half-timbered farmhouses
with steeply sloping thatched roofs, the barnyards
filled with chickens pecking in the dirt.

Nicole refused to be impressed. Instead, she
fumed.

Short of throwing herself out of a car traveling
more than seventy miles an hour, there was little else
she could do except watch the passing farmland. Or
study André Montiard.

The breeze teased at a curling lock of his chocolate-brown hair above the dark line of his brows. His
nose was aristocratically straight, his jaw firm and
lightly shadowed by a heavy beard. Faint squint lines
fanned out from the corners of his eyes, particularly
noticeable when he smiled. She guessed him to be in
his early thirties, a hunk by almost any standard—
hers included, she reluctantly admitted.

Why a guy like this would have to kidnap a woman
to marry him was totally beyond Nicole's understanding. She would have far more easily imagined
women standing in line for the honor. Particularly
since he seemed to have tons of money. Which galled
her all the more.

In her experience, people with money were arrogant, demanding, snobbish and convinced they could
buy anything they wanted. She ought to know, raised
as she had been in the heart of Beverly Hills, the
poorest kid in town.

André eased the shift into a higher gear and applied more gas to the throttle. He liked driving fast. He always had. Having a beautiful woman in the car was an added bonus. Nicole LeDeaux definitely qualified.

Her complexion had a glow to it that made him think of sunshine and roses. So did her scent, so light and fragrant, it was as though she'd just walked through a summer garden. In contrast, her hazel eyes sparking with fury suggested there might be a few thorns lurking behind her petal-soft lips.

A man would be well advised to tread softly, he mused, knowing he rarely took his own advice when it came to women.

The fact that he had studiously avoided marriage for a good many years, then committed the act in such an impulsive way, was a bit out of character, he admitted. Still, it seemed as if his instincts had been damn good. If he had to snatch a bride from the cathedral steps, who could have asked for more than a beautiful princess?

He was definitely looking forward to getting better acquainted. That one kiss had been like an appetizer. He was eager to try a full-course meal.

Not that he expected her to stick around once the election business was settled; it only made sense she'd want to go back to her life. Strangely, that realization hurt more than he cared to admit.

The car tires showered gravel and dust into the air as he turned sharply onto an even more narrow lane.

He down-shifted and they roared up a gently rising hill.

Holding on for dear life, Nicole caught glimpses of the peaceful surrounding farmland; given her circumstances, the pastoral scene was not at all soothing.

The car crested a ridge.

There before them, at the very top of the hill, stood a huge manor house glistening white in the sunlight. Of Palladian design, the three-story structure was graced with a portico of heavy columns, and windows dominated the view in every direction. Nearly a palace, it looked as if it had leapt off the pages of *Architectural Digest*.

A tiled drive circled to the front of the house past neatly trimmed lawns and carefully tended flower beds bright with summer color. André brought the car to an abrupt stop beside the brick porch. When he switched off the ignition, rural silence pressed in on Nicole's ears. Only the ticking sound of the Ferrari's engine cooling marred the silence.

"Welcome to the House of Montiard."

"It's beautiful," she said on a sigh. "Is it a museum?"

His laugh was low and soft and rich with warm undertones. Casually, he rested his arm on the back of her seat. "Some might call it so. I call it home."

Home? The thought startled her. "Why did you bring me here?" She was acutely conscious of his fingers toying with the strands of her flyaway hair and the intense look in his dark eyes. With an effort, she forced aside a growing sexual awareness that fluttered low in her body. This was neither the time nor place to topple head over heels for some guy she'd just met. Who had, incidentally, kidnapped her.

"Where else would a man bring his wife?"

"You've got to stop saying that."

His rakish smile lifted the corners of his mouth again. "We'll have luncheon in the garden. Then I will at last explain all. In every way possible, I intend to satisfy your curiosity."

Nicole had the distinct feeling that he had more in mind to satisfy than simply her curiosity. "It'd be better if you'd call a taxi. I have some business appointments scheduled for this afternoon," she lied, for she'd simply planned to browse the shops around the public square. "Antique dealers. They've probably already called the hotel to confirm the time and are wondering where I am." Unable to hold his questioning gaze a moment longer, she glanced away.

"Ah, my dear, beautiful princess, you do not lie at all well. For that, I shall be eternally grateful, I assure you."

Her gaze snapped back to meet his. "I *do* have to get back to town!"

He placed the back of his fingers alongside her neck and slowly slid them down the sensitive column to the spot where she knew she had a small strawberry-shaped birthmark. André's touch was so extraordinarily intimate, she drew a quick breath. Her heart kicked up a faster beat.

"Let us talk first," he said in a husky whisper. "Over lunch."

The implications of what might happen after the meal so alarmed her, she practically leapt out of the car.

Only the appearance of an old woman coming out the front door preceded by a pack of yapping dachshunds stopped Nicole from racing back down the lane they'd just driven up. In a flurry of eager barks and wagging tails, the dogs surrounded her, sniffing at her ankles and weaving their chubby brown bodies between her legs so that if she moved at all she would no doubt trip over one of the dogs and fall flat on her face.

In an agile motion, André was out of the car and halfway up the steps to the house. *"Grand-mère,* come meet who I have brought home." Affectionately, he kissed his grandmother on the cheek, cupped her elbow and helped her down the remaining steps into the chaos the dogs had created. Though the woman's face was deeply creased by wrinkles, her silver-white hair was impeccably styled. Her black dress was deceptively elegant in its simplicity.

"Have you been up to mischief again, young man?" Smiling, her eyes twinkling with surprising youthfulness, the old woman shook the silver handle of her walking stick at André.

"Every chance I get, *Grand-mère,*" he admitted.

She laughed, a scratchy, frail sound. "Just like your father."

Looping his arm around her narrow shoulders, and squeezing gently, André said, "*Grand-mère,* I would like you to meet Nicole—my wife. King Stanislow's long lost heir. Nicole, may I present Madame Montiard, the most important woman in my life."

There was a moment of heavy silence. Even the dogs stopped their incessant yapping, as though they understood a momentous announcement had just been made. Certainly, Nicole didn't know quite what to say or do. She couldn't run away; that would be rude. She'd been raised to believe rudeness toward her elders and betters was the eighth deadly sin. Yet she desperately wanted to deny she was anyone's wife, most particularly the wife of a man who had kidnapped her. And she certainly hadn't intended to masquerade as royalty.

Madame Montiard recovered first. Extending her thin arms wide in welcome, she said, "At last! I feared my wastrel grandson would never find a woman who suited him. Far too fussy, that boy of mine. And a princess. How very nice." Tears pooled in the old woman's eyes, moving Nicole by the sheer force of her emotion to step into his grandmother's embrace. She smelled of sweet lilac talc. There was little more to her fragile body than skin and bones.

Nicole swallowed hard. She remembered the feel of approaching death in her arms, the final months of her own beloved grandmother's life. *"Madame,"* she whispered, the word constricted by the tightness of her throat brought on by a flood of childhood memories. The first seven years of Nicole's life had been filled with a brightness she'd almost forgotten.

"We must have a celebration," Madame Montiard announced as she stepped back to examine Nicole, holding her hands for just a moment.

The dachshunds renewed their efforts to chew off Nicole's sandals.

"We'll have lunch in the garden, *Grand-mère.* With a little bit of father's own special champagne. Would you like that?"

"Oh, yes, that would be nice." The hand that patted his dark, rugged cheek was gnarled, the covering of porcelain skin, paper thin and lined with veins. But her smile was radiant. "You have done well, son of my son. She is lovely."

Heat flushed Nicole's cheeks.

Madame Montiard turned to lead them up the steps. As though of one mind, the dogs followed suit, hurrying after her into the house through the massive double doors.

As Nicole reached the reception room with its high coffered ceiling and sparkling chandelier, she finally found her voice. "You've put me in a totally impossible position," she whispered to André. "Either you tell your grandmother this whole wedding business is a farce, or I will."

"Be patient, Princess. *Grand-mère* has a weak heart and we wouldn't want to cause her any undue stress."

No stress? What did he suppose she was experiencing?

For a kidnapper's lair, the Montiard home was a treasure trove of exquisite art and sculpture. Before she had a chance to run after the departing Madame Montiard, who was presumably arranging for lunch in the garden, what looked to be an original Flemish tapestry caught Nicole's gaze. Nearby there was a *secrétaire* that looked to be two hundred years old, its marquetry unmarked.

From where she stood in this grand reception room, the two wings of the manor stretched out in perfect symmetry. Rich marble columns of variegated alabaster guarded an impressive stairway that led to the upper floors. Following André down the open length of salons, sculpture galleries and libraries, Nicole's keen eye caught a glimpse of an ornate table clock resting on a gray marble-topped, gilt console table.

Just one of these items would have made a significant stir among collectors in Beverly Hills. To see them all in one house was mind-boggling.

The garden was equally striking. Serpentine paths lined with a bright array of perennials led to an artificial pond. One entire area was given over to roses that bloomed in such profusion their heady scent filled the raised terrace onto which André had led her.

"I trust you approve," he said as she stood in dumb-struck awe.

"Very impressive." She shifted her gaze from the garden to the man who had brought her here. He was impressive, too, very much the lord of the manor, his hands clasped behind his back, his pride evident in the set of his chin and his wide-legged stance. In spite of his easy smile, there was an aura of power about him along with a heavy dose of confident sexuality.

With shocking awareness, Nicole realized André Montiard and his world represented everything she had always wished for. Here she would not be little Nikki LeDeaux, the housekeeper's daughter who'd been rarely seen and never heard in the big house in Beverly Hills.

And she hated herself for the rush of envy that cut through her midsection like a jagged knife.

Unaware of Nicole's inner turmoil, André began speaking in his low, cultured voice. "The Montiard family was granted the lands in this valley sometime during the Crusades. I gather one of my ancestors was handy with a sword and managed to make it to the Holy Land and back in one piece. Quite an accomplishment in that day and age, I imagine. Except for a few brief interruptions when assorted armies passed this way, there has always been a Montiard living on this site."

"That's all very interesting, but what does it have to do with why you brought me here?"

He gestured for her to be seated at a circular glass table shaded by a wide white-and-yellow umbrella. Too agitated to sit, she refused with a quick shake of her head.

"The prime minister of our country, Hendrik Meier-Wahl, is a ruthless man who will stop at nothing to protect both his power and his financial interests," André explained. "He rules with an iron fist and the people suffer because of it."

"With all due regard, it doesn't appear the Montiards have suffered a great deal."

He shrugged noncommittally. "Our wealth nearly matches his and is arranged so that for the most part he cannot gain control over us."

"This Meier-Wahl is the man you said was planning to kidnap me?"

"Apparently you announced as you came through customs that you are the heir to the old Margolis throne. Word spreads quickly through our small country, and most of the government employees, one way or the other, owe their allegiance to Hendrik."

"He got a late-night phone call?"

"Most likely. Either Hendrik or a member of his staff. You recall the car that stopped in front of the cathedral steps?"

Nodding, she shivered at the memory. As he went on to describe Hendrik's likely plan to kidnap and drug her into cooperation, possibly even marriage, she felt as if she had slid down Alice's rabbit hole.

"Why didn't you simply call the police?" she asked. "Surely they could have protected me."

"He owns them, too." In a gesture that radiated tension, André shoved up the sleeves of his turtleneck, revealing muscular arms lightly covered with dark hair. "Last year a man tried to blow the whistle on their operation. He met with an unfortunate and fatal accident."

"You suspect murder?"

"I suspect Hendrik capable of doing anything he wants to, and being able to get away with it."

Nicole had the feeling she was in way over her head. Murder plots were hatched in films, not real life—*her* real life. She knew people who had been mugged, and one friend had even had her car hijacked in the middle of a major L.A. intersection. But she didn't know anyone who had experienced the threat of murder.

A maid appeared in a black dress and starched white apron with a matching cap. She dipped them both a quick curtsy, along with a shy smile at Nicole, and proceeded to set the luncheon table for three with crystal goblets and silverware that gleamed in the sunlight.

When the maid vanished back into the house, Nicole said, "I appreciate you trying to save me from this Hendrik person, but I think the best thing would be for you to take me back to the airport. I'd like to get out of here as soon as possible." She could always carry on her hunt for antiques in France or Germany. Choosing to visit Margolis had evidently been rather foolish.

"But our people need you, Princess."

"That story was just some nonsense my grandmother made up when I was a kid to make me feel like I was worth something. I don't even know what made me mention it to that surly customs man."

"Then you don't think you are the heir?"

"Not likely."

"Strange." His eyes narrowed slightly. "Then how do you explain the fact you carry the mark of Margolis?"

She blinked, an unsettling feeling coming over her. Vague memories of her grandmother's words tugged at the back of her mind. "What are you talking about?"

"The customs man may have noticed it, too, and that is why he called Hendrik." André touched her just below her left ear, that sensitive spot he had caressed so intimately in the car. "The birthmark that resembles a crown with three points. It's quite distinctive. According to legend, every royal heir since the eighteenth century has carried that mark."

"That's ridiculous." She took a step back. "What you're talking about is hardly more than an oversized freckle." Which was, in fact, very much like the freckle on her mother's throat.

"A very attractive one, I might add." He grinned. "In this case, however, it carries a much deeper meaning. And poses a certain amount of danger to you, whether or not you remain in Margolis."

Feeling suddenly weak in the knees, she took the seat he had previously offered. She rubbed her fingertips to her temple. Her brain was about to short circuit. There was no way she could be a true princess, surrounded by court intrigues, no less.

André sat down next to her, taking her hand in his. Although he may have meant the gesture in a reassuring way, she was instantly aware of the power he held over her, and her reaction to his polished sexuality. She noted the length of his tapered fingers, their strength, and how a smattering of dark hair covered the back of his hand. His olive skin contrasted sharply with her fairer complexion, doubling her sense of his power. The roughness of his palm chaffed against her softer flesh.

"This man who died—was he close to you?"

"My older brother, the rightful heir to the Montiard fortunes. Christian had a rather devoted sense of responsibility to our country, unlike myself. Until recently, of course. He thought that he could make a difference if he took on Monsieur Meier-Wahl." André's dark eyes glistened and he squeezed her hand. "Unfortunately, the same accident in which he died also killed his wife and child."

She felt a quick surge of compassion. "I'm sorry. I truly am. But your loss has nothing to do with me."

"A returning princess could help set things right again. The people might listen to you and have the courage to throw Hendrik out of office."

She forced down a rising sense of panic. Playing on her sympathies was a devious trick. She was going to need all of her wits if she had any hope of escaping his velvet trap.

Slowly she withdrew her hand.

He studied her a moment. "I gather you do not approve of my efforts to rescue you, or my hopes for our country."

"The wedding wasn't exactly what every girl dreams about."

"It was in a church."

She made a derisive sound. "I would have preferred the cathedral... with a man of *my* choice."

"You do not find me an acceptable groom?" His dark eyes mocked her.

"No." A good many other women would, she was sure. But not Nicole. Not under any circumstances.

"Perhaps you already had some other man in mind for that role in your life?"

"Not exactly." She saw a flash of what could have been relief in his eyes. But it was gone so quickly she couldn't be sure.

"Ah. Then you find me lacking in some way."

"I wouldn't say that precisely. After all, I don't even know you. But you are quite different than the kind of man I had in mind."

"I would welcome a more detailed explanation of my shortcomings." One side of his mouth quirked in an arrogant, amused smile.

She ground her back teeth. "Look, if and when I marry, I'll do it voluntarily, and it will be to a nice, steady kind of guy. Maybe a mechanic. Or an accountant. Somebody who comes home every night at five and goes bowling Thursday nights with the guys. And on Sundays we go on family picnics." In a glance, she took in the massive house and sprawling gardens. "I don't belong in a place like this, and I don't want to live the way you live."

"Not even temporarily?"

There was that damn carrot again, she realized, tempting her to accept what she knew couldn't be hers. "No. When I agree to a marriage, I expect it to be a permanent arrangement."

"My father managed to enjoy four different wives." He shrugged easily. "Permanence does not seem to be one of the virtues of the Montiard men."

"That's precisely why I am not interested in getting involved with you or your family's problems." Nicole's mother had dreamed about a prince who would save her from scrubbing floors and serving tables; it hadn't worked.

Bursting through the terrace doors, Madame Montiard herded her dachshunds into the garden. "Do behave yourself, Alphonse. You, too, Mimi. And Edgar! Tsk-tsk. Such naughty children," she admonished the dogs. The animals' nails clicked noisily across the tiled terrace as they raced pell-mell on their stubby little legs to investigate Nicole once again.

Laughing, she gave each of the six dogs a quick pat before they could devour her sandals. When she caught André's amused expression, she felt a renewed sense of unease. Nicole knew she didn't dare relax her vigilance. Marriage to a total stranger was not a part of her plan. At the very least, as a way to stop this Hendrik fellow, it seemed a bit extreme.

ALL DURING LUNCH, Nicole held her tongue, waiting for the right moment to tell her would-be grandmother-in-law the whole wedding was a farce. The moment never came.

When they finished the meal, the pretty young maid unobtrusively removed the luncheon plates from the table, replacing them with dessert dishes. From a cut-glass compote she carefully served each of them a lemon pudding topped with a drizzle of raspberry sauce.

"Thank you, Katja," Madame Montiard said. The girl curtsied, then silently vanished back into the house.

"Madame Montiard, I don't want to upset you," Nicole began, frustrated by her inability to speak her piece, "particularly if your health is frail, but this so-called marriage—"

"Is quite a wonderful surprise. I think we should arrange a small party. Something intimate for a few of our friends." She shifted her attention to her grandson. "Don't you agree, André?"

"Absolutely, *Grand-mère*." The corners of his eyes crinkled.

"You don't understand—" Nicole objected.

"Perhaps we should include one or two of your political associates. That might be wise with the election coming soon." Madame Montiard allowed one of the dogs to lick a bite of pudding from an extra spoon that had been placed on the table.

"What election?" Nicole asked, her head swiveling to André.

"I am standing for election to parliament. If all goes well, I shall be prime minister."

"Prime min—" She choked. A man who kidnapped women off the streets?

Ignoring her, André redirected his attention to his grandmother. "I shall leave you in charge of the social calendar, *Grand-mère*."

"There isn't going to be any party!" Nicole objected. "I'm not going to be here that long."

"Now, now, child." Waving away the dog, Madame Montiard covered Nicole's hand. A slender, extraordinarily beautiful diamond bracelet circled her bony wrist and each of her fingers sported either an emerald or ruby mounted in a gold ring. The total worth of the jewelry would have supported Nicole until social security kicked in. "I know all new brides are nervous at first about meeting their husband's friends, but you mustn't worry. They'll love you, just as I do.''

"That's not the point."

"Grand-mère can be quite stubborn when she sets her mind to it, Nicole. I suggest you resign yourself to enjoying whatever she has in store for us."

Madame Montiard smiled at her grandson. "After you get settled, I do so hope you two young people decide to start your family right away. I don't want to rush you, of course. And I certainly wouldn't think of interfering with anything so personal. But I just don't know how much longer I might have left on this earth, and it would be nice to meet the next Montiard heir."

Nicole choked. *"Heir?"* The woman was suffering from selective hearing, not a heart condition. "But there hasn't been a real wedding," she objected.

"You two were a bit hasty. But we will rectify that in due time."

Leaning forward, a devilish gleam in his dark eyes, André said, "A boy would be nice but a girl will do."

Nicole had a sudden flash of what it would take to produce the offspring he had in mind, but quickly blocked the thought from her mind.

"No," she groaned, a headache threatening at the base of her skull. "You don't understand. I don't belong here."

"Of course, you do, dear. You are now a Montiard." The older woman stood, which created a new flurry of activity among the short-legged dachshunds. "I fear it is time for my afternoon nap. Doctor's orders, you know."

With a gracious smile, she swept away from the table, the dogs trailing behind her like a swarm of eager children.

Nicole nailed André with a look that was meant to kill. "I'm not going to let you do this to me."

Chapter Three

Nobody listened to her.

Certainly not André. After lunch he went blissfully off to conduct business in town, assuring Nicole he would pick up her suitcase at the hotel and be back in time for dinner.

Not even the maid, Katja, paid any attention to Nicole's protests that she was not married to André or anyone else. The girl simply showed her to the master bedroom suite, dropping curtsies every other step, giggling, and addressing her as "Your Highness."

Nicole was fit to be tied.

Forget that the master suite consisted of two airy rooms plus a dressing area that by itself was as large as her entire apartment in Los Angeles. She was not going to be distracted by the ornate Boulle writing table with exquisite inlaid mother-of-pearl and gilt-bronze mounts. Nor would she take time to examine the delicate enamel box set with cameo miniatures.

And she certainly wasn't going to give any thought to the draped bed that looked as if it might be an original Chippendale.

The fact was, there were no locks on any of the bedroom doors. None. She'd checked.

No way was she going to stick around the House of Montiard unless she had double padlocks on everything between her and that man.

He was the devil incarnate. Too sexy, too damn sure of himself for any woman's peace of mind. He threatened her with the same kind of silky threads that snared a fly in a spider's web. Every time he looked at her, she felt as though she were being undressed, exposed both physically and emotionally. His eyes were the source of his power, she concluded, dark and compelling, with a wicked glint that made her feel more feminine than she could have thought possible.

Her breath came hard and fast, and her heart accelerated as she slipped out a door she'd found at the back of the house. She would escape from this prison without bars, despite the appeal it had for someone who had always dreamed of living in such a place.

Imagine. To be a real princess. With riches at her fingertips, power and influence over the lives of others with only the generous wave her hand. And a darkly handsome prince at her beck and call. Impossible dreams. All of them.

Checking over her shoulder every few steps, she edged past a row of garages that must have housed half a dozen cars, then she ducked to run down the sloping hillside. Loose dirt caused her to slip more than once in a puff of white dust. Vines with blooms looking like morning glories reached out to twine around her ankles like Madame Montiard's dogs. At one point Nicole slid downhill into a berry patch, coming away with a good many scratches on her arms and a few black stains on her linen skirt.

When she reached the main road she mentally breathed a little easier, although she was still panting and her heart was racing about ten zillion beats per minute. She'd simply hitch a ride to town, she told herself, and then to the airport. By nightfall she'd be out of the country. André could keep her suitcase as a souvenir.

The first car roared past her in a cloud of the fine chalklike dust that seemed endemic to the countryside. She could understand the driver's hesitancy to stop. She must look a mess, her hair in total disarray, her skirt and blouse stained and dirty. But after the second and third vehicles ignored her, as well, she began to get angry. Next time she heard a car coming she'd stand right smack in the middle of the road, she vowed. They'd stop. Or run over her.

TO MASK his excitement about finding and marrying the heir to the throne, André forced himself to stroll casually through the newspaper offices of the *Margolis Times*. He made his way past rows of cluttered desks, the occupants of which were working at computer terminals or talking earnestly into headset phones. The newspaper publisher was in Hendrik's pocket but André knew a sympathetic reporter. Robert von Helman would be delighted to run a story about the marriage of Princess Nicole to the leading opposition candidate for Hendrik's job. Polls had shown support for the two men and their respective political parties, was almost equally divided. With any luck, nostalgia for the good old days would put André and his fellow Labor party candidates out ahead.

He smiled to himself. Acquiring a beautiful bride was an unexpected fringe benefit. He imagined if he applied himself, he would be able to overcome Nicole's resistance and avenge Christian's death at the same time. After all, giving up his carefree bachelor's life—even temporarily—would increase his credibility with the populace.

He had no long-term expectations for his marriage to Nicole. Although there might be temporary pleasures they could both learn to enjoy.

Stopping at the reporter's desk, he leaned over the computer terminal to greet his friend through a haze of cigarette smoke. "Good afternoon, Robert. How is your Pulitzer prize-winning novel coming?"

"Ah," Robert said with a smile that squinted his eyes nearly closed. "I have my hero trapped by the renegade CIA agent in the middle of Africa, the natives are throwing poisoned darts at them, and the lions are on a rampage because the heroine has innocently stolen one of their cubs. I think the plot is coming along nicely, thank you.''

"Definitely a winning concept." The corners of André's lips twitched. Fortunately, Robert was a much more competent journalist than writer of fiction. "I have another story for you that will benefit us both."

As André related the events of that morning, he watched Robert's interest spark and hold in his gray eyes. His cigarette remained untouched in the ashtray until André paused for his reaction.

Lighting another cigarette off the first, and frowning, Robert paused for effect before recalling his country's history. "King Stanislow of Margolis died November 18, 1915, by assassination, confirmed by reliable eye witnesses, but his body was hidden and never found. He had one son—" he raised his bushy eyebrows meaningfully, interrupting the flow of facts his retentive mind could conjure up on a moment's notice "—named Nicolas, who had already fled the country because of the impending war. It was assumed he had gone into hiding, but in the chaos of several million refugees it was impossible to track his whereabouts. Neither he nor any of his family members was heard from again. It is possible, given the politics of the time, Nicolas would have remained in hiding for some years. Or perhaps, he simply died."

"She has the mark of Margolis on her neck." A perfect target for a man's kiss, André thought, recalling the brush of his fingers on the soft flesh of her throat. "And her hair color is the same as the old king in his portrait at the castle museum." A rich shade of auburn that reminded him of autumn leaves in the vineyards.

"All of that might be nothing more than coincidence."

"She was told as a child she was the heir."

"Your marriage to this woman seems a bit extreme to gain a political advantage."

André met his curious gaze with a smile. "I like to think of the act as a pleasurable expedient."

Robert exhaled a stream of smoke and coughed. "I will run your story because it will prick Hendrik right where it hurts. Meanwhile, I will put my sources in the States to work trying to confirm her claim from that end."

"You have my undying thanks, Robert."

"Just be sure you buy a copy of my book when it is published."

André laughed. "You have my word."

"One last warning, my friend. I have heard rumors…little more than whispers. There has been talk of reviving the monarchy. A splinter party has been formed."

André didn't give much credence to the threat. Winning even a single seat in parliament required more than a few scattered votes. But a wise man would remain on alert.

As he left the building, he spotted Hendrik's press secretary talking with the managing editor. He did not intentionally avoid Marlene Marquette, his late brother's sister-in-law and a woman who had relentlessly pursued André when they were both too young to know their own minds.

On the other hand, he felt no great urge to go out of his way to greet her. In addition to being a member of the opposition's camp, there was something slightly unsettling about the young woman.

WHO WOULD have dreamed the farmers of Margolis would still be using horse-drawn wagons? Nicole mused. And wasn't it just her luck an onion farmer had been the one traveler on the road kind enough to give her a lift. She'd been trying not to breathe deeply for the past hour or so, but it wasn't working. Her eyes burned and so did her lungs.

"It is that Meier-Wahl who has us in such a fix," the farmer continued his complaint, his accent so thick she could sometimes barely understand him. "He raised the taxes on petrol so high we cannot even afford fuel for our tractors. And all of the money goes only to line his pockets."

"Then why don't you throw the bum out on his political ear? That's what we do in the States." At least, that was the theory.

"Ah, it is much more easy for you." He flicked the reins across the horse's rump. The aging animal gave very little response, plodding steadily down the dusty asphalt road, his hooves clomping in weary rhythm. "You have had democracy for two hundred years. We are babies at such things. Only since the Great War. That is why it is so good you have chosen this time to return to our country."

"Me? Return? I've never been here before." *And I don't plan to come back.*

The farmer smiled, revealing stained, uneven teeth. On a human scale, he looked even older than his horse. "Ah, Princess, we know you have come back to help Monsieur Montiard."

"I'm not a princess!" She rolled her eyes heavenward, her gaze sweeping helplessly across a cloudless blue sky. "I'm an ordinary American trying to get started in the antique business. Why is that so hard for all of you people to understand?" The entire country suffered from selective hearing.

"Perhaps," he said softly, his narrow shoulders dejectedly folding in on themselves, "because we need help so much. André Montiard is a fine man in his way, and he has been a good landlord for those of us who are tenant farmers. He cares about the people. The land, too. The country will have its best chance if he can become prime minister."

"I can't imagine why you think that." An experienced kidnapper hardly seemed qualified for the job.

"You do not know him so well as those of us who live in Montiard County. You only see him as—how do you say?—a player with the women."

"You mean, he's a playboy?" She could more easily believe that description than to think of him as the leader of Margolis.

"Yes, it is for that reason no one takes him seriously." His shrug spoke of stoic acceptance of his lot in life. "If you do not help us, who will?"

Nuns could not have laid the heavy weight of guilt on Nicole's shoulders more effectively. She really liked the old farmer and appreciated his kindness, for all the good it might do either of them. "I'm truly sorry. I'm simply not the right person to—" She looked up to discover the House of Montiard looming on the hillside right above them. "You've been driving around in a circle!" she accused. He was supposed to be taking her into town.

"Yes, *madame.* I would not want Monsieur Montiard to lose his bride so quickly. Not when she is such a beauty." He gave her a guileless grin that grated on her conscience. For heaven's sake, the farmer saw André as a paragon of virtue, and she'd been trying to escape!

A car roaring past them distracted Nicole from the string of vindictives that came to mind. The black Citroën wheeled hard in front of the wagon, spraying up a cloud of white dust before it slid to an abrupt stop. The horse shied, then ground to a halt.

She was horrified to recognize the same car that had approached her earlier that morning at the cathedral. The one André had warned her about. Hendrik's men. And they meant her no good, she realized, as two burly thugs dressed in dark suits appeared out of the vehicle, one of whom she recognized. The guy with the broken nose. They approached the wagon from either side, effectively blocking any escape route.

In a moment of longing, she looked up at André's house on the hill. If she could just get there she'd be safe. Surely the brutes wouldn't pursue her that far.

But there was no chance at all she could make it up the steep slope to safety before they caught her.

Fear and indecision immobilized her as she frantically sought some other means of escape. "Do something," she pleaded to the farmer. "They're going to kidnap me."

The farmer tugged on the reins, trying to back the horse and wagon, but the poor old nag didn't budge.

As a last resort, Nicole was ready to start throwing onions at the thugs when she heard another car coming down the road. A horn blared. The two men halted, swiveling their attention to the approaching vehicle.

She turned to follow their gaze, relief washing over her at the sight of a shiny maroon Ferrari convertible roaring in their direction, bearing down on them fast. When it pulled to a stop beside the wagon, she didn't hesitate for a moment. She leapt to the ground and gratefully threw herself into André's car. He sped away, leaving Hendrik's buddies in a cloud of dust shaking their fists in the air. The farmer seemed unconcerned by the entire affair.

The pounding of her heart filled her throat. "Thank Heaven, you came back." From the grim set of his jaw, she suspected André was furious with her.

Gripping the wheel tightly, André forced himself to remain calm. When he had called the house and discovered Nicole had fled, a sudden sense of loss had filled him—mixed with a fair amount of anger, he admitted. Then he had realized she could still be in danger from Hendrik's men. That thought had driven him to find Nicole as fast as he could. Her safety was his responsibility, and their hasty marriage had placed her in an extremely vulnerable position.

It took him a moment before he was cool enough to speak. "I am disappointed in you, Princess."

"Oh, please, don't start that again. Those men scared me to death."

He wheeled sharply up the drive to the house. "Did you think so little of the Montiard hospitality you felt it necessary to run away?"

"I'm not very fond of being held prisoner against my will. Nor am I thrilled by the prospect of being kidnapped by rival political factions."

"Do you now understand there is reason for my concern for your safety?"

"I've figured out this Hendrik you've told me about must be one tough customer. Katja was nearly in tears because he got her boyfriend fired. And that farmer hates him."

"So do many of our people. The unrest is growing rapidly. I intend to give my country another option."

"Civil war?"

"I am a man of peace, I assure you. Enough blood has been shed already."

She gave him a sharp look at the surprising determination in his voice. There might be more depth to the man than she had realized. Perhaps the farmer perceived André more accurately than she did.

They reached the top of the hill. Down-shifting, he roared past the main entrance to the house and circled to the back where Nicole had earlier discovered the row of garages. One of the doors opened electronically to his command. Without slowing, he whipped the car into its stall and brought the Ferrari to a stop alongside an equally impressive Rolls-Royce town car. Beyond that was a spotlessly restored Jaguar, vintage 1970.

Nicole drew a shaky breath. André appeared to do everything at high speed. She suspected he'd also seduce a woman in the same way, racing past her defenses before she fully realized the approaching danger. From what the farmer had said, and from what she had easily surmised, André had far more experience with women than she had with the opposite sex.

Sitting easily behind the wheel, his wayward lock of hair brushing his forehead, his black turtleneck sweater tugging across the breadth of his shoulders, he was the most virile man she had ever met. Unsettlingly so. She imagined his chest would be furred with the same dark hair that roughened his muscular arms. A texture she wanted to investigate for the sheer erotic pleasure of touching him.

For a fleeting moment she wished he could be the one to teach her all the mysteries she'd been afraid to explore. But that was a foolish thought. He wanted to use her for his own political gain. Under other circumstances he wouldn't give someone like her a second glance. Why should he? She wasn't all that much to write home about, and she certainly lacked the sophistication he probably expected in his women.

Not that she totally lacked admirable qualities. She could spot a phony Tiffany vase at a hundred paces. Managing her way through the antique auctions where it was dealer-eat-dealer was a piece of cake. She simply didn't know how to handle herself around a man like André Montiard.

Drawing another deep breath, she said, "So you're telling me that trying to beat Hendrik at his own game by kidnapping me has been for noble reasons."

"I would like to think so."

She eyed him skeptically. "What is it you really want of me, André?"

He returned her a slow, appraising look, his gaze sliding across her features, settling briefly on her lips, then returning to her eyes. "I only ask that you pretend our marriage is real—which it *is* as far as Father Thomas and the church are concerned.''

"Only because the priest is interested in your contribution," she stated, but he ignored her observation.

"I need two months. Until the election. With you on my arm, I can sway enough votes to elect a majority of Labor party candidates to parliament."

"So you can be prime minister in Hendrik's place."

"That is our plan. There are fifty-one districts represented in the Margolis House of Commons. If the Labor party can elect twenty-six members, we can oust Hendrik."

"Aren't you a bit young to be ruling a country?"

He gave her an appraising look. "I think you will find at thirty-six, I am at my prime."

She caught his double meaning and flushed. At least he was now being honest about why he had married her. On all counts, though she preferred to ignore the sexual connotations. "You really think you'd be better for the country than he is?"

He lifted his shoulders in an easy shrug. "I could not be much worse. Our economy is stagnant because of his heavy-handed ways at a time when many countries are moving forward. Most of the blame can be laid at Hendrik's feet."

Nicole suspected that was true. Certainly the farmer thought so. Still, there were some major personal issues that needed to be clarified.

"You're only talking about a marriage of convenience, right?" she asked. "A chance to use the fact that I may be the heir to the throne?" To each of her questions, he nodded his answer. "That's all you have in mind?" Not a few tumbles in that huge draped bed upstairs?

"All other matters we can allow to take their natural course."

That sounded like he was hedging but she let it slide for the moment. "What about my business? This isn't a vacation for me. I'm scheduled to open my shop in less than three months. The lease papers are all signed and ready to go, and I've got a line of credit arranged." Which would put her so far in the hole she was risking bankruptcy even before she got started. "If I don't have a successful buying trip, I'll never make it."

He pondered that for a moment, his hands moving thoughtfully over the steering wheel in a caress gentle enough to have been meant for a woman.

"I could introduce you to a few local dealers," he offered. "For a friend of mine, they might be willing to discount their merchandise."

"Really?" Oh, Lord, she could sense temptation rearing its ugly head again. A two-month-long shopping spree, all at discount prices, plus a chance to play the part of a real-life princess.

"It would be worth a try."

It would, indeed, if the local dealers had even a few items as exquisite as Nicole had spotted in

André's home. Her success back in the States would be guaranteed. She'd have customers flocking to her from all across the country. The possibilities were unlimited. "Well, if you're sure . . ."

A triumphant grin creased his cheeks and created an unsettled feeling low in Nicole's belly. She might well have just made a serious tactical error.

"I knew you would agree."

"Not so fast," she warned, holding up her hand and mentally backpedaling. "There's one more thing I want made perfectly clear."

Still smiling, he lifted a questioning eyebrow.

"I want locks on my bedroom door. Very solid padlocks. And I'm the only one who has a key."

His laugh started as a low rumble in his chest, rose insistently until he threw back his head to give full rein to his amusement at her expense. "As you wish, Princess. But you should be forewarned. I am the kind of man who enjoys a challenge." His smile broadened and he drew the back of a single finger along her cheek, lowering his voice seductively. "Particularly when it comes to women."

Nicole shuddered. Somehow she should have known that.

Chapter Four

Marriage was a great deal more difficult than he had anticipated, or at least, marriage to an *unwilling* woman.

Tugging the sash to his lounging robe snugly around his waist and looping it at the front, André listened grimly to the muted sounds coming from the adjacent bedroom. She was moving around in there. Getting undressed. Probably slipping into the lacy negligee he had found spread neatly across her bed at the hotel. He had stuffed the handful of sensuous fabric into her suitcase, his fingers lingering among the soft folds as he imagined the feel of his hand sliding the silk along the curve of Nicole's hip, caressing her narrow waist, and finally lifting the gown past the contour of her full breasts. The image had tightened the muscles of his groin then and gave him the same reaction now.

For all the good it did him.

She had hardly looked at him during dinner. Only *Grand-mère's* steady stream of conversation about plans for a celebration party had saved the meal from being a total disaster.

Then Nicole had fled the table, mumbling excuses to escape upstairs to the bedroom where she actually bolted the locks he had been forced to hastily install.

Locked out on his wedding night! It was damn hard on a man's ego. And didn't do much for his reputation, either. He would have to swear the staff to secrecy if he was going to carry off this charade until election day.

Granted, he had negotiated the arrangement with Nicole. Their marriage, after all, was to his political advantage. But damn it! He was attracted to Nicole. *Seriously* attracted, so much so, his body ached with the tension. Even his teeth felt on edge.

Clenching his fingers into fists, he realized he was not used to being told no. Given his attraction to her, it was reasonable to assume she felt something in return. Certainly she had responded with considerable passion to their kiss at the church. He could still recall her sweet flavor and how she had leaned into him with an astonishing eagerness, particularly under the circumstances.

He paced across the room to the open French doors where a soft, summer breeze stirred the curtains, bringing with it the scent of roses. A fragrance much like Nicole's.

The light from her bedroom window spilled a square of color onto the dark garden below. A man should not be kept from his bride on their wedding night, he mused. Not that he would consider taking what she was unwilling to give. He was anxious, however, to renegotiate certain aspects of their arrangement. An impossible task with locked doors between them.

For a moment he contemplated the narrow balcony with its low balustrade that ran along the side of the house between the two bedrooms. If he happened to arrive at her open window with a fresh bottle of champagne and two glasses, how could his bride possibly refuse him entrance?

DRAWING THE BRUSH through her hair, Nicole realized this was the bedroom she had dreamed about as a child, a boudoir fit for a queen. Even the vanity table with its scrolled legs and the low, padded bench on which she sat were just as she had imagined them. In the small Beverly Hills apartment above the garage that had served for servants' quarters, she'd let her youthful fantasies have free rein; make-believe was far better than reality.

Nicole blinked back tears that welled in her eyes. Her childish dreams had no more substance than her current situation. She must not get used to this kind of elegance, to the rich, brocade bed covering, to satin sheets, or to the presence of exquisite porcelain figurines that seemed to be everywhere in the house, making her fingers itch to caress them.

And she could not, under any circumstances, envy that others took such gracious living for granted.

As though he were a part of her fantasy, something she'd conjured up out of a dream, she caught a glimpse of André in the mirror. In his deep burgundy lounging robe with its black satin lapels, he looked the epitome of polished sophistication. He leaned with easy, masculine grace against the frame of the open French door, eyeing her with an indolent smile that echoed the same invitation as the champagne and glasses he held. *Let me seduce you,* they said in a devilishly tempting voice. *Let me carry you away from your dull and humdrum existence.*

She closed her eyes against the image, pressing her fist against her stomach as though she could block the cravings that rose up within her.

"Good evening, Princess."

She went very still. This was no fantasy. He was in her room. Dark and seductive, and he'd gotten past the locks on her door!

She whirled and leapt to her feet. "What are you doing here?"

"This is our wedding night." He strolled lazily into the room. "I thought we should spend at least some of it together."

"No. That wasn't our agreement." She backed toward the opposite corner.

"Only for a toast, my dear. To seal our bargain."

"We had champagne at lunch. Wine at dinner. That's good enough." She certainly didn't need to get tipsy, not when she was locked inside a room with the one man she desperately wanted to keep locked out.

"A nightcap, then. That is all I ask."

But that wasn't all he had on his mind. Not by a long shot. His eyes were a little too dark, his gaze all too blatantly filled with masculine approval as he perused her from head to toe. The sheer robe she wore proved small defense against his warming scrutiny. Her skin flushed and she folded her arms across her waist.

"Perhaps I didn't make myself clear earlier. The reason I demanded padlocks on the doors was to keep *you* out."

He placed the crystal champagne glasses on a table and began working the cork free from the bottle. "Surely you are not afraid of me."

"Since you were the one who kidnapped me originally, perhaps you can understand why I'm experiencing a certain amount of anxiety." Not to mention other emotions she didn't wish to explore too deeply.

"I have already assured you, you are quite safe with me."

Like chickens are safe when the fox is in the hen house. "Look, André, this has been a rather stressful day for me. I'd like to call it quits and go to bed. Alone," she added pointedly.

He cocked an eyebrow, then slid his gaze to the huge bed with the velvet drapes tied back at each corner. "Pity." The cork popped.

She flinched, as much due to the unspoken meaning in his look as to the sound of the cork.

He poured the wine, the clear liquid drifting into the glasses with a sibilant whisper. In the light from the table lamp, a shower of effervescence appeared, forming miniature rainbows.

Lifting the glasses, he walked toward her. At a subliminal level she registered menace in everything he did—the danger of his greater strength, if he chose to use it, and the danger of her vulnerability born of envy for the life-style he led. Deeper still, she was aware of her own fascination with the dark tuft of hair visible at his open collar, and the way evocative shadows played across his features, emphasizing the strong lines of his jaw and angled brows.

"Indulge me?" He offered her a glass.

His dark gaze issued an invitation to concede more than a drink of sparkling wine. "Is it possible that the men in this country don't understand the meaning of the word no?"

The corners of his lips trembled slightly with the threat of a smile. "A genetic flaw I hope you will learn to appreciate."

The man was a hopeless flirt, that's what he was. "Oh, all right," she agreed, stifling a responding smile. "One toast."

When she accepted a glass, André raised his in salute. "To us."

"To our bargain," she countered.

As he sipped the wine, André studied Nicole over the top of his glass. She would be a foolish woman to trust his intentions. He suspected she was neither imprudent nor as naive as she let on. In spite of her efforts to maintain a mental distance, her flushed cheeks gave away her sexual excitement. Perhaps even she was unaware of the subtle signals that radiated from her, messages he skillfully translated— the way she fingered the lacy collar on her gown, drawing his attention to the ivory column of her throat, the somewhat breathless rise and fall of her breasts.

Still, there was the remote possibility at some other level she was actually frightened of him. Or embarrassed by him seeing her in a gown sheer enough to reveal the faint shadow of her rosy areolas hiding beneath the fabric, a thoroughly enticing sight. Almost as enjoyable as watching unobserved while she brushed her long, auburn hair until it shone in the lamplight like a gilded drape across her shoulders. Perhaps she lacked the experience to play the flirtatious games so common among the women he had met . . . and enjoyed. An intriguing possibility.

"Well, that's it, then," she said after a single sip of wine, dancing away from him to place her still full glass on the table next to the bottle. "Good night."

His lips quirked into a smile. "You are dismissing me so soon?"

"As I said, it's been a long day."

In two long strides, he was at her side. He ensnared her wrist before she could escape, suddenly aware of the delicacy of her slender bones, as fragile as a fine piece of porcelain. She looked up at him with wide, startled eyes and he heard her suck in a frightened breath. The top of her head came to just above his shoulders and he felt as though he were towering over her.

"I assure you, Princess," he said, the roughness in his voice testament to a sudden wave of tenderness that swept through him, "although I find locked doors little more than a nuisance, if and when I decide to bed you, it will be because that is what we both want. Can you believe that?"

She nodded dumbly.

"Good. In that case, I will steal one single kiss to conclude our celebration, and bid you good-night."

The objection Nicole intended vanished beneath his lips; they molded to hers for an instant, warm and insistent, inflaming her with the quickness of a lightning bolt. Then they were gone, leaving her breathless and feeling she'd had a glimpse of something quite wonderful she'd never even known existed.

She watched André exit the same way he had arrived, a dream evaporating into the night, and she could almost believe the entire incident had been only her imagination. Except there were still two glasses on the table beside the champagne bottle, and her lips still felt moist with his distinctive flavor, and quivery with need for an encore.

Sitting heavily in the nearest chair, she wondered how on earth she would ever be able to avoid his sensual onslaught for even so short a time as two months.

THREE DAYS LATER, as she sat in the high-ceilinged salon of a haute couture's showroom, the memory of André's brief good-night kiss still had the power to send a rush of heat curling through Nicole's midsection. He sat next to her in one of several velvet chairs scattered around the room as they watched tall, lanky models present dresses for Nicole's consideration. Meanwhile, the woman in charge fluttered about, curtsying and mumbling "Your Highness" every chance she got, and kowtowing to André.

A thousand times Nicole had walked or driven by the exclusive stores on Rodeo Drive in Beverly Hills, wondering what it would be like to shop there. She'd pictured herself arriving in a BMW, the valet helping her out of the car, and the salespeople hovering around her. She'd had no idea of how drugging the aura of wealth could be. And she didn't want to get too used to the feeling; withdrawal would be painful.

In contrast to Nicole's reactions, André was taking the attention in stride. No doubt he'd never had anyone glare at him because he didn't belong.

Sitting easily in a chair that looked almost too small, he was a formidable presence in his dark, hand-tailored suit and fine silk tie. Only the persistent lock of misbehaving dark hair that curled across his forehead softened his high-powered image. And his cocky grin that appeared at the most unexpected moments, doing something erratic to Nicole's heartbeat.

He hadn't visited her room since that first night. Though, Lord help her, she'd lain awake a good many hours listening to the sounds of him moving around his quarters and half hoping he would appear. Not that she would have, even on the penalty of severe torture, admitted her secret longing to anyone else in the entire world.

During the days, André had been away from the house, doing whatever it was politicians do, and in the evenings he only had time to dine with Nicole and his grandmother, then off he'd go again, making Nicole feel thoroughly useless. She was getting better acquainted with Madame Montiard and her dogs than she might have liked. Sweet lady that she was, André's grandmother dropped the names of the rich and famous like a trail of bread crumbs. In the process, Nicole had learned André maintained a rather active social life that annually took him skiing in San Moritz, scuba diving in the Caribbean, and sunning himself on the Costa del Sol, all of his adventures in the company of people with just as much wealth as he possessed. Which was clearly substantial. For good measure, his acquaintances included a few heads of state, a royal here and there, and a smattering of Hollywood movie stars considered marginally acceptable in Madame Montiard's crowd.

Only once in the past three days had Nicole managed to slip away to explore a flea market filled with wonderful antiques. At her urging, the butler had taken her, and then he'd been severely reprimanded by André for his efforts. It seemed Nicole's husband still feared for her safety.

Sighing, she studied the slinky brunette model wearing a Dior original, a royal blue number with an off-the-shoulder blouse and dramatic fanlike sleeves worn above hip-hugging satin pants.

"I can't afford to buy any of these outfits," she protested in a whisper to André. "Just one of them would use up my clothing budget for the next two years." And most of the designs she wouldn't be seen in outside of her own home. Beyond that, her pride wouldn't allow her to accept such an expensive gift from any man. Not even her "husband."

"Do not trouble yourself, my dear. You are my wife now. You may have as large a clothing allowance as you wish." He eyed her with a half smile. "For as long as our marriage lasts, of course."

"Allowance? That sounds like I'm a child who doesn't have to work for her money."

"But of course not. Why should you? I have never worked for a single franc in my life. The Montiards hire managers to take care of their money."

The life-style he led so naturally continued to astonish Nicole.

Leveling him a determined look, she said, "I've earned every penny I have, and I'm darn proud of it. I think you'd have a better understanding of money, and your country's economy, if you had to get your hands dirty once in a while. Do a little honest labor. Maybe that would make you a better politician, too."

"For you, my dear, I would work my fingers to the bone." His gaze swept over her in a teasing caress. "But it does seem other activities would provide a more pleasurable use of my time."

She stood—because to sit there a moment longer, knowing what he was thinking, and *thinking* exactly the same erotic thoughts herself, would have made her squirm. And she had far too much pride to let him know just how his innuendos and wicked good looks affected her. "Let's go to a real store, where *real* people shop, and I can afford to pay my own way. Simply because your grandmother wants to have a wedding party doesn't mean I have to spend a fortune on a dress."

"As you wish, Princess." Standing, he placed his hand possessively—*warmly*—at the small of her back. "We shall mingle with the peasants, if that is what you prefer."

"I do." She certainly didn't belong in a showroom where she couldn't afford even a single sleeve from one of the elegant dresses, much less the whole gown. She also didn't belong in André's life, pretending to be the heir to a throne that didn't exist. The whole idea was ludicrous. Yet she craved the chance to walk across the thick carpeting of the showroom and inhale the scent of luxury—fine fabrics, polished wood, and the lingering trace of rare perfumes. She chided herself all the time she indulged her weakness.

In spite of her best intentions, a small "Oh" escaped her lips as a model in an exquisite wedding gown appeared from the dressing rooms. The dress was all white lace and frills, with a train that could only be shown off properly in a cathedral ceremony. Just another one of those foolish dreams that persisted in tugging at Nicole's imagination, she reminded herself.

Handing the doorman a generous tip, André escorted Nicole outside. The morning had been a new experience for him. Since the year he had reached the age of majority, women had cajoled him into buying them expensive gifts. Now, for the first time, a woman had actually declined his offering. A situation that left him both pleased and puzzled.

Perhaps American women were less concerned about money than he had thought. Truth was, the designer gowns paled in comparison to Nicole's natural beauty.

Within a few minutes, André had driven them to a small apparel shop on a side street near the main square in San Margo. Instantly Nicole felt more at home. At least the price tags wouldn't cause her credit card to do a meltdown.

"Perhaps this one, Your Highness," the solicitous shopkeeper said as she pulled a bright red gown from the rack. The neckline appeared to plunge nearly to the navel.

Nicole declined with a quick shake of her head. "I don't think so."

"But *monsieur* would like, no?"

"*Monsieur* would like very much," André conceded, his lips quirking into a smile, "but *monsieur* would need a very large stick to drive off every man in Margolis. Perhaps something a bit more conservative?"

Fighting a flush that heated her cheeks, Nicole sorted through the row of evening gowns, finally picking three to try. When she modeled a form-fitting gown in a muted green silk, with a modestly low neckline, the glint of appreciation in André's eyes told her all she needed to know.

Stepping into the dressing room to change, she reached for the zipper at the back of her neck. Fingers more deft than hers were already there.

A low, raspy voice at her ear said, "You will be the loveliest bride Margolis has ever seen."

"André," she gasped. Shivers sped down her spine. "You're supposed to be waiting—"

"I fear I must rush you. We have a date with a friend of mine. An antique dealer—"

She turned so quickly she found herself in his arms, his fingers splayed across her bare back as he lowered her zipper. His body was so close, she caught the leathery scent of his after-shave. A heady, masculine aroma. Awareness settled low in her body, of his heat, his penetrating dark eyes, and how much she wanted all that he represented.

"You've finally arranged a meeting?" she asked, ignoring the tight sensation that squeezed at her heart.

"Did you doubt my promise?"

"Of course not. I just didn't know when—"

"Today. If you can drag yourself away from all this luxury." His mocking smile crinkled the corners of his eyes.

"You'll find most women would be delighted to shop in a store this nice."

"Not the women I know. This small shop would be far beneath them. Indeed, in that regard you are quite unique." He placed a soft, yet startling kiss on her forehead. "As I am finding you are unusual in many ways."

Her heart did a little somersault and she pressed her palms to his unyielding chest. "Out with you," she ordered, fighting the quiver in her voice. "I can't hurry while you're still standing there." So close, his

warm breath stroked her already heated cheeks in a
gentle caress.

SUMMER HEAT hung heavy and moist in the air. In
spite of the breeze that swept past the fast-moving
Ferrari, beads of perspiration dampened the back of
Nicole's neck. A tapestry of pewter-colored clouds
stretched across the sky, promising little relief from
the humidity.

"I wish you had allowed me the honor of pur-
chasing your new gown," André said as they sped
down a country road. He had removed his jacket and
his shirt collar was unbuttoned, his tie tugged loose.

"All I ask of you is a chance to find some good
antique bargains in exchange for this little charade
you've cooked up."

He gave a slight shrug as the car eased into a turn
past a picturesque farmhouse. "Each of us must get
something we want from this 'marriage of convenience.' Is that not so?"

"I don't feel as if I've contributed much so far."

With a raised eyebrow, he implied a few sugges-
tions she didn't wish to consider.

"To your political campaign," she quickly added,
ignoring the startling thought that his blatant efforts at seduction would be more than acceptable if
their marriage were real. Which it wasn't.

"Holding me a de facto prisoner in your house
isn't likely to gain you many votes. American presi-

. dents have learned to put their wives to work. At the very least, you're missing great PR opportunities."

"In truth, you have already caused quite a stir among the populace and gained for me considerable attention in the press. Rumors about your return scatter like the seeds of a dandelion, forcing people to vie for invitations to our wedding party Saturday night. They all wish a chance to meet you."

"Gracious, I hope I don't disappoint them."

"That would not be possible, Princess." A smile crept up his face, creasing his cheek. "The longer they are required to wait, the more appreciative they will be of your beauty and the more eager they will be to seek out your favor."

"And cast their votes for you and your party?"

"Your debut has been carefully orchestrated to have the greatest impact possible on the campaign."

"Why do I get the feeling I'm little more than a puppet on your string?" A feeling she didn't particularly enjoy.

In the process of turning onto a secondary road, he failed to respond to her question, but the thought continued to trouble Nicole.

The village antique shop was a quintessential junk store. To the tinkling sound of a bell over the door, the store owner appeared from the back room, sweeping aside a beaded curtain with an easy swipe of her hand. Wearing a scarf wrapped around her head, and a colorful skirt, she looked as old as most of the merchandise in the musty, crowded room.

"Ah, Montiard, I have been expecting you." Like an aging dancer, she made her way gracefully through the clutter. The long row of silver bracelets on her arm jangled. "I have been reading your charts, and your signs are in ascendancy."

"Does that mean the Labor party will win the election?"

"For that information, young man, you must place but a few coins in my hand—preferably gold ones."

He laughed and turned to Nicole to make the introductions. "Petra is my favorite Gypsy fortune-teller, as well as a seller of whatever she can lay her hands on. She always has good news for me, *if* I am willing to pay the price."

"And for you, Montiard, the price is only half as much as I charge that misbegotten Meier-Wahl." She made an angry, guttural sound. "He will run us all into bankruptcy if he is not stopped soon."

"Perhaps my wife will be the key to our success."

With a smile, Nicole said, "I'm very pleased to meet you."

Petra refused the handshake she offered, instead turning Nicole's hand over so she could study her palm. Struggling against an uneasy feeling that prickled the back of her neck, Nicole forced herself to keep a businesslike smile on her face.

"Excuse me," she said, futilely trying to retrieve her hand, "I'm really here just to look at any antiques you might have. For my store in the States."

Her expression intent, Petra shifted her attention from Nicole's hand to the strawberry mark on her neck, her gaze studying the imperfection with a skeptical eye. "Quite amazing, Princess," she said in a breathy sigh.

Nicole shuddered. The look in Petra's eyes was too private, as though she were seeing through Nicole to the past, or on into the future, and stripping away her masquerade of royalty. Nicole sensed the woman knew the truth—that she was a fraud.

André looped his arm possessively across Nicole's shoulder. "Why don't you tell us how long-lasting our marriage will be?"

After a brief hesitation, Petra returned her attention to Nicole's palm. "Ah," she said after careful examination, "your marriage line makes it clear you shall enjoy much happiness. And from your womb three fine children will be born."

"Three?" Nicole choked, and a flush raced up her neck. Why was everyone so anxious to get her pregnant with André's child—a real trick since she had no plans to make love with him. This fortune-teller was way off the mark, unless somewhere in Nicole's future there was another man....

To her dismay, Nicole instantly rejected the thought of any other man in her life. Then cursed herself for her folly. No way could she build a life as a Montiard. A housekeeper's daughter simply wasn't suited.

"If you don't mind, I'd like to browse around a bit and take a look at what you have."

"Of course, Princess. For you I will not even inflate my already exorbitant prices." She laughed, a low, husky sound, breaking the tension that had filled the air like an electrical charge.

Nicole escaped into the narrow aisles that separated the cluttered merchandise. She noted a chipped figurine sitting side-by-side with a priceless enameled box, an original oil painting tucked in next to a poor copy. There seemed no rhyme or reason to the shop. Nor were her thoughts making any sense.

In her mind's eye she kept imagining three beautiful children with André's dark eyes and his dimpled grin. The possibility of making that picture real was a fanciful thing, thoughts that nagged at her even as she studied a collection of knickknacks that were only pre-World War II. She felt her breathing accelerate, her heartbeat grow heavy against her ribs, and she forced herself to calm down. She was *not* going to think about having André's babies.

André sidled up to her. "Perhaps this is what you seek." With a teasing grin, he showed her a ghastly ceramic lamp made in the shape of a purple elephant, its raised trunk designed to hold the light bulb.

She choked back a laugh. "I don't think that's quite what my clients would be looking for."

"No?" He studied it a moment longer with mock seriousness, his head cocked at an angle. "Perhaps you are right. Although you must concede, it is unique.''

"Definitely one of a kind," she agreed as he wandered off again.

She'd barely gone back to her own explorations when he appeared with a huge beer stein.

"Now I've got it!" he announced. "How could your clients possibly resist this?"

Swallowing a giggle, Nicole shook her head. The stein was made in the shape of a naked woman with the largest breasts she had ever seen. It would easily take a quart of beer to fill each one. "Certainly a collector's item, but not exactly what I was looking for."

His shoulders slumped dejectedly, but the corners of his eyes crinkled with humor. "This antique business is more complicated than I realized."

Nicole knew that wasn't true. From the clothes he wore and the way he lived, she suspected André had impeccable taste.

He had a lighthearted sense of humor, too, she mused, a trait she'd always valued in others. Probably because she tended to be overly serious.

She shot him a look across the width of the store. Lord, she was beginning to like being with the man— and she didn't dare do that.

"Over here, my dear," he called to her.

Reluctantly, she made her way through the maze to his side and he proudly lifted the lid of a floor-standing Regina music box, an instrument that was probably made around the turn of the century. Of course, André had found the most priceless item in the entire shop.

Nicole drew an admiring breath. The rosewood, though dulled by the lack of care, seemed to be in good condition, and the mechanism looked to be intact, including a circular metal disc punched with musical cues. Unable to resist, she ran her hand reverently across the wood finish and carefully examined the enameled country scene painted on the front. "It's lovely," she whispered, excitement at such a find bubbling within her like a glass of fine Montiard champagne.

"I thought you might like it."

"I know a wonderful workman in Santa Monica who could refinish it. And if it still works—"

"Let's try." He fiddled with the mechanism. A moment later the tinny strains of "My Wild Irish Rose" filled the antique store.

André thought he had never seen a woman quite so beautiful. Nicole's eyes glistened with excitement, turning in the dim light to rich green, as though she had been kissed by an Irish balladeer. A smile played at the corners of her lips. He suddenly hoped someday soon that same smile of pleasure would be intended for him.

The thought brought him up short.

Perhaps it was her hesitancy he found so intriguing. Women generally fell at his feet—or more correctly, fell into his arms—with the least little encouragement. To please them, however temporarily, had been his pleasure. His father, after all, had been his role model. Indeed, even his legendary brother, a man who had been on the verge of truly changing the country for the better, had managed a few discreet affairs during his brief marriage. As had his wife, André thought grimly.

Nicole, he sensed, would not tolerate a wayward husband.

Not that this new awareness changed in the least his desire to break down the barriers she had erected during their brief marriage of convenience.

Chapter Five

By the time they exited the antique shop, the first few drops of a summer rain were spattering here and there to darken the cobblestone street. Nicole had purchased several items in the store, all at good prices, she admitted. In turn, Petra had agreed to have the merchandise delivered to the House of Montiard for later shipment to the States.

"I wish Petra hadn't told us about the family that had owned the music box," Nicole said, trying to shake a persistent feeling of unease.

"A good many of our people have fallen on hard times in recent years." André cupped her elbow as they crossed the street to the car. "Gypsies among them. It is hard for the men to get honest work and everyone is convinced all of our crime is because of Gypsy thieves. Old prejudices die hard in this country."

"But to be forced to give up a family heirloom in order to feed their children?" She shook her head in dismay. "It seems so terribly unfair. Almost criminal."

"Ah, the Princess of Margolis is experiencing guilt for taking food out of the mouths of Gypsy babes. You could always order them to eat cake."

"Don't tease me, André. I just made a really smart business deal and somehow I'm not feeling all that good about it." Nor was she feeling good about Petra's misguided prediction for her long-lasting marriage to André, or the way the woman had so easily gotten under her skin with her penetrating gaze. The Gypsy fortune-teller knew something, she thought uneasily. Something that boded trouble for Nicole.

André opened the car door, eyeing Nicole with interest, and noting how her skirt rode up her thigh as she settled into the leather seat. A woman with good legs and a soft heart, he mused. Interesting combination. The more he got to know her, the more he found Nicole LeDeaux quite fascinating. Pity about the lock still on her door. He had been avoiding her for the last several days in the fond hope her resistance would weaken; so far his plan did not seem to be working.

"Shouldn't we put up the top?" she asked.

He glanced toward the threatening sky and, as though in perfect insult, a drop of rain plopped right on his cheek. He frowned. A heavy rain this time of year could be disastrous for his tenant farmers.

Placing both hands on top of the closed door, he leaned forward, bringing his face close to Nicole's where he could catch her sweet scent. "Have you ever helped with a haying, Princess?"

"You mean, like on a farm?"

"Exactly."

She shook her head. "I'm a city girl through and through."

"Then I have a treat in store for you, love. We are going to go help a friend of mine bring in his hay before it gets too wet and is ruined." He dropped a kiss on top of her head, inhaling the floral scent of her shampoo. He repressed a groan. Abstinence was definitely not his style. "Think of it as another opportunity for you to mingle with the peasants." And maybe a chance for him to catch Nicole off guard long enough for a few passionate moments in a stack of sweet-smelling hay.

"I don't know anything about farm work," she protested as he hurried to snap the convertible soft top in place.

"Jean Paul has a pair of old horses anyone can learn to drive. You will be fine."

André slipped into the driver's seat and twisted the key in the ignition, enjoying the distinctive roar of the engine. As he pulled away from the curb, he noted a Citroën in his rearview mirror falling in line a block behind him.

Damn! He hadn't expected to be followed to the village. Distracted as he had been with Nicole, he had not even bothered to check his car for signs of tampering. He should have.

He tapped the brakes lightly. They felt fine, just the right amount of peddle, a firm, steady grip on the road. But his carelessness could prove deadly if he did not remember to watch himself. Hendrik had a heavy hand when it came to political opponents.

Glancing in the mirror again, he could only hope Hendrik's men would do nothing foolish that might endanger Nicole. Although his arrangement with her was only temporary, he did feel a strong obligation to protect her during the interim. Then, like both his mother and his childhood sweetheart, she would no doubt seek a liaison with some other man.

For a moment, a childish anger at prior desertions twisted through his chest, and he forcefully shrugged off the feeling. Women could not be relied upon. The Montiard men had learned that lesson more than once.

THE HORSES were no trouble. Not exactly high-spirited, the pair of sturdy animals trudged up and down between the rows of cut hay with only the encouragement of an occasional flick of the reins to keep them moving.

Nicole could even handle the overpowering scent of freshly cut hay, and how the tiny bits and pieces wormed their way down her neck and under her shirt.

The problem, as usual, was André.

He'd changed into a blue work shirt and an old, worn pair of snug-fitting jeans that rode low on his lean hips and hugged his muscular thighs. If she had thought he looked dangerous in his black turtleneck sweater, and professional in his business suit, now he simply took her breath away. Like a chameleon, he seemed to be at home anywhere. And in each costume he was all the more devastatingly handsome.

She found it quite surprising that he had a set of work clothes stashed with the farmer, as though he often dropped by to help out. Why would a man who claimed he didn't believe in working for a living be so intimately acquainted with manual labor?

And he was. He tossed hay into the wagon with an ease that only came from experience and muscles accustomed to the task.

When he looked up at her, grinning foolishly, his hair dampened by the continuing rain, she had to sternly remind herself André was the wealthy landlord who lived up on the hill. She, and people like the farmer, Jean Paul, were only pawns in his life, to be moved about as he saw fit.

"The rain is starting to come down harder," he said. "Maybe you should wait in the barn while we finish."

The old farmer working the opposite side of the wagon grunted his agreement.

"I'm fine," she said. "I don't think I can do much damage to these clothes you found for me to wear."

The jeans she wore were about three sizes too big, and the cotton shirt hung to her knees.

"I don't want the heir to the Margolis throne catching cold on my account."

"Actually, the rain feels pretty good." The drops weren't coming too fast and the temperature was still uncomfortably warm, making the air steamy. "As long as I can help, I'll stick around."

"I told you, Jean Paul," André called across the wagon, "my wife is born of true nobility."

"Humph. Then she deserves better than you, my friend." The words were said with quiet affection, the old farmer obviously pleased André had come to help him with the harvest. And had brought Nicole along, as well. He had welcomed her with a big smile that shifted his weather-worn features like Christmas morning brightens the face of a child.

"You are probably right, old man, but you do not have to slander my reputation in front of my bride. Better to let her find out the truth on her own."

"And what is the truth?" Nicole asked, teasing him with a haughty twist of her shoulders.

"That there is not a finer fellow in all of Margolis," André answered before Jean Paul could reply.

She laughed in spite of herself. "Nor one with a larger ego?"

"Quite possibly."

He rested the tines of his pitchfork in the ground for a moment, long enough to give her one of those wicked, seductive grins that sent a surge of unadulterated lust curling through her midsection. Worse yet, it reminded her again just how much she was beginning to like the man.

She'd known from the first that she was physically attracted to André. But she'd known other men who were handsome, and a few with equally silvered tongues. Resisting their advances had never been difficult. An icy look put them off. Or a curt reply. Not so with André. Nothing seemed to slow his relentless pursuit.

As his indolent, dark-eyed gaze swept over her, she knew with a certainty that she was due for the battle of her life, mostly with her own conscience. Everything he said or did built toward an inevitable intimacy between them. His desire to buy her clothes, his uninvited presence in the private dressing room of the dress shop. Or in her own bedroom, for that matter. The way his hand frequently found the small of her back, or how he looped his arm across her shoulders in a thoroughly familiar gesture. Every time they were together, he persisted in slipping inside her personal space. Even making her laugh.

Darn it all! She was beginning to like it. And him.

Her fingers closed so hard around the reins, the tired horses came to a halt.

"Something wrong?" André asked.

Nicole gritted her teeth. "Not a thing." Except her heart seemed to have a mind of its own. She had never *allowed* herself to consider finding a man who was fabulously wealthy, sophisticated and charming. A prince. That fantasy had been her mother's downfall. Twice. Once with the unnamed man who had fathered Nicole. The second time with the owner of the house where her mother had served as housekeeper and sometime mistress.

The same kind of man would be Nicole's Waterloo, she realized, aware of the unhealthy longing she had to rise above her humble beginnings. Ordinary folks. That's who she was, current pretensions to royalty aside. There was no way she belonged in a clique that included jet-setters and heads of state.

Then why was she so strongly drawn to André? she wondered. Did she harbor some genetic condition that forced her to repeat her mother's mistakes?

Exhaling a shaky breath, she clicked the reins over the horses' rumps. She would not admit, even in the deepest recesses of her mind, that she wanted, desperately, to belong to the world in which André moved so easily or to be with him in every intimate way possible.

By the time they'd filled the wagon, the rain had become a heavy downpour, sheets of water spraying across the landscape like an impenetrable veil. Thunder rumbled in the distance and lightning flashed.

Nicole hurried the anxious horses into the barn. Water steamed from their coats in an aromatic mist, and their chests heaved from exertion as they moved uneasily with each new clap of thunder. One of the horses nickered softly, as though asking for reassurance from her partner.

Through cracks in the leaky barn, filtered light dappled the interior, casting a muted mosaic of light and shadow across horse stalls and hay-covered floors.

She wiped the rain from her face, then twisted the water from her long hair.

"Do you often have summer storms like this?" she asked.

André lifted his arms to help her from the wagon. "Not often."

She slid from her perch on the hard wooden seat into his embrace, instantly aware of her mistake. They were too close. His hands encompassed her waist in a tender vise, and slid higher until his thumbs pressed gently against the underside of her breasts. She shuddered at the sensations that coursed through her. Heat. Wanting. Undeniable desire as quick and potent as the storm building outside. Urges she fought to deny.

Dirt and sweat streaked his aristocratic features, the result of hard labor she could appreciate. His leathery after-shave mingled with the scent of damp hay, a rich, earthy combination. She was aware of his lean body, the breadth of his shoulders and the brush of her thighs against his. His dark hair shone with raindrops, the light catching the moisture in silvery streaks.

She heard a soft moan that could have been his. Or was it hers?

Beneath her hands she felt his biceps ripple and flex, setting up an echoing sensation low in her traitorous body.

She didn't want this.

Feigning disinterest, she slipped away from his grasp on legs gone suddenly rubbery. Idly she patted the horse's rump, trying to ignore the heavy beat of her heart against her ribs and the surge of hormones that had caused her breasts to feel extraordinarily full.

André exhaled the breath he had been holding. He was definitely losing his touch. He had been so fascinated by the way Nicole's eyes had widened in surprise, and her irises darkened with arousal, he had failed to take advantage of the moment. Simply holding her, feeling the soft swell of her breasts, anticipating, had been too pleasant to rush the moment.

And then the chance was gone. Like a dream, she had fled before he had been able to put substance to his thoughts. She was the first woman he had ever brought to Jean Paul's farm, a citadel of safety André had found as a child. Her presence buoyed him, making his obligations feel a little less heavy as they rested on his shoulders, and making him long for something he never thought he would have.

Next time, he vowed, he would not delay the kiss he had so much desired.

"You seem quite at home on this farm," Nicole said, still visibly fighting to steady herself.

"I probably spent more time here as a boy than I did up at the house."

She slid a questioning gaze his direction. "Why?" He was standing with his thumbs hooked in his jean's pockets, like an arrogant Margolis cowboy, and her eyes were drawn to the way his hands framed the soft, faded denim tugging across his lean hips. Erotic images assailed her and she swallowed hard.

"My best friend is Jean Paul's son. Sebastian and I were inseparable as children."

The older man appeared on cue, giving André a quick squeeze of his shoulder while his expression remained impassive. "And I would not let the boy laze around my farm while the rest of us worked. As it was, he set a bad example for my son."

"Sebastian was the one who thought up all the crazy schemes," André defended himself.

"And who was it that went along with his plans?" he groused, beginning to unhitch the wagon team. "Pouring white glue in Madame Turon's milk pail. Shame, shame on you."

A hidden smile creased the farmer's leathery face and he gave Nicole a wink that spoke volumes about the affection he and André shared. "You two go inside," he ordered gruffly. "*Maman* has made you some tea and sweets. Though why she should use up our sugar on the likes of you I will never know."

"Peach tarts?" André asked eagerly.

He grunted. "What else would a foolish old woman make to bribe the landlord?"

With a pleased, almost boyish grin, André said, "Nicole and I will help you take care of the horses, you cantankerous old man. Then we will all go have some of *Maman*'s pastries."

Amazed at the close relationship between André and the farmer, Nicole did what little she could to help put the animals into their stalls. She dipped a bucket into a bag of oats, then dumped the feed into a trough. The smell of horses, leather and hay she found strangely pleasant—natural—and with André's presence, like an aphrodisiac; she tried not to think about that.

As she and André hurried through the pelting rain toward the ancient farmhouse, she asked, "How is it you're so close to these people?"

He shrugged. "Because they have never asked anything of me except to let me be myself."

His painful admission startled Nicole. Could she have misjudged him? she wondered. Surely he didn't want to be anything other than a wealthy playboy. Then she realized the answer to her question didn't make any difference. He was still using her for his own political ends and planned to discard her when his election was accomplished. That was their arrangement. She needed to focus on acquiring as many antiques as she could at the lowest possible prices. That way her future would be in her own hands.

As she stepped onto the farmhouse porch she decided not to pursue why that thought depressed her.

IN THE COZY warmth of the kitchen the delectable scent of fresh-baked pastry permeated the air. André leaned against a counter, amused at the way Jean Paul and his wife, Anna, fussed over Nicole. They had instantly adopted her for a daughter, as if they did not have enough children and grandchildren of their own.

"Really," she protested, sliding her plate to the middle of the old wooden table, "the tart is absolutely delicious, but I simply couldn't manage another bite. Certainly not a second piece." A little dollop of sweet cream clung to the corner of her lip in an intriguing way. André nearly groaned aloud when she licked it off with the rosy tip of her tongue. She looked particularly sexy in Sebastian's work shirt, he mused.

The fact that she was so thoroughly at home in this rustic farmhouse amazed him, particularly when she looked equally a part of the House of Montiard, with all of its straitlaced elegance. He wondered what was in her background that allowed her to become a part of either world with such easy grace. Instinctively he had known she would fit in with his friends as no other woman had.

"But we must do something so very nice for André's bride, no?" Gray-haired, rounded and plump, Anna hovered near her guest. "And you are so very—how do you say?—skinny. We must put some meat on these bones so you do not blow away, is that not so?"

"*Maman,*" Jean Paul warned from his place at the table. "Do not say such things."

Nicole's cheeks flushed. "I don't think there's much chance of my blowing away, whatever weather you get around here."

The storm had moved past the farm, the thunder now rumbling farther to the east. Rain settled on the roof in a steady, monotonous drip.

"Then you must let me teach you to make these tarts for André. They have been his favorite since he was a small boy."

"I confess I'm not a very good cook."

André crossed his arms in front of his chest and hooked one ankle over the other. "If I had known you cannot cook I might not have married you in such haste."

"You weren't exactly interested in taking the time to get acquainted," she remarked with an accusing glare.

"I am more than eager now."

The color on her cheeks deepened.

Good, he thought, meeting her hazel eyes with his own amused expression. She had no trouble reading his meaning. They were managing to get better acquainted by the minute, whether she liked the idea or not.

Anna patted Nicole's shoulder reassuringly. "The tarts are easy, my child. You will learn in no time at all. And André has a leg which is hard to fill."

"You mean, he has a hollow leg?" Nicole asked, the corners of her lovely lips quivering with the effort to prevent a smile.

The single light above the kitchen table flickered and went out.

Anna looked up, scowling at the offending light fixture. "Bah. It is the storm. Always we lose our electricity. The government should do something."

Frowning, André straightened. The short hairs at the back of his neck prickled. The storm hadn't caused the power loss. The worst of the weather had blown past an hour ago, just as they had finished the haying.

Shifting his position in a way that wouldn't alarm the others, he glanced out the window. A breeze twisted the spindly branches of a weeping willow, but except for a few chickens pecking along the ground in the backyard, it was quiet out there. Too quiet.

"Where's your old dog, Jean Paul?" he asked as casually as he could. Anxiety rasped across every nerve ending.

The old man lifted his narrow shoulders in a noncommittal shrug. "If you would come around more often you would know we had to put her down more than a month ago. Her bones ached until she could no longer move."

"Sorry to hear that." Though it did explain the absence of a barking dog if someone had come onto the property. And there was someone prowling around. With a sixth sense honed since the death of his brother, André was sure of it.

Hendrik's men.

Only vaguely aware of the continuing conversation between Anna and Nicole, he slipped out of the kitchen to check the front rooms of the house. The place was as familiar to him as his own home. The narrow hallway. A closed door into the downstairs bedroom where Jean Paul and Anna slept. A rickety staircase leading upstairs to Sebastian's room and those of the other children, long since grown and gone. A living room dominated by an overstuffed chair where Jean Paul fell into a doze every evening after supper, his pipe in his hand.

Then he saw it. Through the lace curtains that covered the front windows, he spotted a figure moving. Fast. In a running crouch. Coming toward the house.

An instant later, glass shattered. A lamp toppled over with a splintering thud.

André acted instinctively and still had only a moment to shout "Get down!"

A deafening explosion rocked the house.

Chapter Six

Nicole registered André's warning too late. The force of the blast had already knocked her to the floor where she'd landed half under the table. She lay there trembling and trying to catch her breath, her hands and face clammy, her stomach unsettled. Only Anna's quiet sobs aroused Nicole from her state of shock.

On all fours, she crawled across the room to Anna's side. The older woman sat with her legs splayed out in a vee, her back against the cupboards. A ribbon of blood oozed down her temple. Tears welled in her eyes.

Nicole snatched a dish towel from the counter and pressed it to the cut so the blood wouldn't drip into her eye.

"Shh, Anna, you're all right. The cut's not deep. There's just a lot of blood." She'd probably struck her head on the counter as she fell.

"My Jean Paul," she sobbed. "Where is my Jean Paul?"

In a quick glance, Nicole saw the farmer struggling to his feet. Though his age-worn face looked pale, and he was a bit wobbly as he stood, he appeared unhurt. "He's fine," she assured Anna. "Your husband is fine."

But, André... Dear God, what had happened to André?

She'd seen him leave the kitchen only minutes ago. After that she'd heard his warning shout, then the explosion.

Fear coiled through her, knotting Nicole's innards. She had to find André!

"Jean Paul, can you hold this towel in place until the bleeding stops? Please." Her voice caught.

She scrambled out of Jean Paul's way so he could take over, then headed out the kitchen door into the rest of the house. An acrid smell hung in the air, burning her nostrils and fueling her fears. She followed a narrow hallway toward the front of the house.

In the fading afternoon light she could only make out a few jumbled shapes in the living room. A chair tossed carelessly aside. Tables overturned. A curtain shifting in the breeze at a window that no longer contained a single pane of glass.

Rising panic constricted her throat. "André?" she called.

A groan.

She whirled toward the sound. Frantically she clawed at an old overstuffed chair, pushing and pulling to get it out of the way. The worn upholstery came apart in her hands. André was alive, she told herself. She'd heard him. For now, that was all that mattered.

She found him curled in a fetal position, his long legs tucked up against his stomach, his hands covering his head. "André?" Gently, she took his hand. His fingers felt warm, his palm lightly callused.

He groaned again, turning slightly.

"Easy. Don't make any fast moves till we see if anything is broken."

In the dim light, she could see his eyes blink open and slowly focus. His fingers closed over hers and a smile played at the corners of his lips. "Ah, my beautiful princess. My own personal angel. Have I died and gone to Heaven?"

Relief washed over her, along with a swell of joy. The man was an incorrigible flirt, even when he had nearly been blown to bits. "Trust me. There's not a chance they'd let you through those pearly gates."

A frown tugged the dark line of his brows together. "Jean Paul and Anna?"

"They're both fine. Anna got a cut over her eyebrow when she fell, but it's not serious."

Blowing out a sigh, he levered himself to a sitting position, wincing as he did.

"You're hurt."

"It is nothing." He rubbed at his arm. "I banged my elbow when I took a dive behind the chair, which is probably what saved my life."

"Do you have any idea what happened? Did a gas heater blow up?" She couldn't imagine anything else that might have exploded like that.

He shook his head. "My guess would be a pipe bomb."

"P-pipe bomb?" Surely her hearing had been affected by the explosion. She still had a ringing in her ears. "You can't mean . . . ?"

"Hendrik's thugs. I was afraid they might do something foolish."

"Foolish?" she echoed on a cry, a new surge of panic threatening. "They could have killed us."

"That was probably the idea."

"Oh, my God... Are they...?" She looked around frantically. "Could they still be out there?"

"They didn't wait around to pick up the pieces. I heard a car drive away just before the thing went off."

The thought of a pipe bomb staggered Nicole. "Is all of this because you're trying to oust Hendrik from office?"

"He doesn't believe in half measures."

Trembling worse than she had before, she sat back on her haunches. "I don't believe this. All I ever wanted was to start my own business. Just a few nice antiques. That's the only reason . . ."

As her voice trailed off into a hiccup, André pulled her into his arms. "I understand, Nicole." Tension and anger lowered his voice a notch, and he fought the urge to seek out and kill Hendrik with his bare hands. "As soon as we can get this mess straightened up, and get Jean Paul and Anna settled, I will take you to the airport. Tonight, if that is what you want."

She lifted her head from his shoulder. "But that would mean..." Her jaw visibly tensed. "We can't let them get away with this."

"I do not want to place you in danger any longer."

"This isn't some undeveloped country in the middle of nowhere. Darn it all, this is Margolis. A *civilized* country. We can't let the law of the jungle rule here." She squared her shoulders. "I'm not going to run simply because some tyrant threatens me. I am, after all—" she lifted her chin a little higher "—the heir to the throne. What would old King Stanislow think if I fled the country at the first sign of trouble?"

Amazed by her bravery, he framed her face between his palms. "You are a courageous but foolish woman." And more fascinating than any he had ever met. More caring, too. When she had raced to his aid, he had seen the depth of her concern in her eyes. Not since he was a very small boy had a woman cared so much that he might be injured. Then one day he'd awoken to find she was gone.

He swallowed back the bitter, hurtful memory. "Go back to America where you will be safe, Nicole."

She eyed him suspiciously. "You're not going to run away, are you?"

"I cannot. My course was set a long time ago." *The day my brother was killed.*

"Then if I can still help you beat Hendrik, I want to stay. For the sake of Anna and Jean Paul, and Petra, and Katja's boyfriend, and everybody else who is suffering because of that jerk. These are *my* people," she said regally.

In spite of himself, he smiled at the noble lift of her chin. But he had to consider her safety first. "Things have gone too far. I am no longer sure I can protect you."

"Then we'll get help from someone else. The police?"

"They won't do anything." Their inquiry into his brother's death had been a farce, a cover-up of the worst kind. Clearly, someone—Hendrik or one of his hirelings—had ordered the police to turn a blind eye.

"Then we'll— I don't know..." He could almost see her mind sorting through options. "We'll call the Cable News Network," she blurted.

If the situation had not been so serious, André would have laughed. "Ah, my naive little princess, what good would television do?"

"We'll get the whole international community on our side. Getting the media involved is the kind of thing people would do at home." She stood, tugging him up with her. "After all, a lost heir to the throne returning to save her native country would make a great story. There'd be headlines in every newspaper in every city in the world. We'd be the underdogs fighting back. Hendrik wouldn't dare harass us. In fact, he'd probably be forced by international pressure to offer protection."

"Interesting concept." But fraught with risks for both of them. "Do you actually intend to claim the throne?"

"No, of course not."

"But you are willing to play the role in earnest?"

"I think it may be the country's best chance. Until the elections are held." She raised her fingertips to caress his cheek, her eyes intense, her forehead pleated with concern. He loved how much she could care. "Isn't it worth a shot?" she asked.

Her determination relaxed a band around André's chest that had been there a long time, as though she had a key to unlock the pain he had kept hidden from public view. "What about us? Our relationship?" Taking her hand, he placed a kiss on her slender palm.

"Well, I guess we go on as we have been."

"With the locks still on the door between us?"

He sensed a moment of hesitation before she withdrew her hand and said, "I think that's best."

"Pity. Still, if you are willing to risk your life for the country, how can I, a lowly subject in Your Majesty's service, offer any objection?'' And he intended to hire as many bodyguards as it took to keep Nicole safe. She was far too precious to risk, particularly when the barriers she had erected between them were beginning to weaken.

In the distance, a siren wailed.

"Somebody must have called the police," he said, glancing out the shattered window at the flashing red light across the valley. "I will see if I can reach Sebastian. Jean Paul and Anna cannot stay here until repairs are made."

"Will they be safe then?" Nicole asked.

"If you and I stay away from the farm," he conceded grimly.

THEY CALLED a hurried press conference for the next afternoon on the causeway over the moat to Castle Margolis. An impressive three-story stronghold, rectangular towers rose at each corner of the structure, and smaller, elaborate twin towers protected the gatehouse. The building was still used for government offices, as well as a national museum, and Nicole felt as though she were a lamb being led to the slaughter.

A light breeze caught the hem of her skirt, fluttering it at her knees. As a concession to her new role, she had reluctantly allowed André to order several new dresses for her, a more elegant gown for the party, and this silk and linen suit, all of which had been delivered to his home that morning. For this appearance, she'd chosen to wear a suit in a light shade of teal. She hoped the color would flatter her on television. She had taken extra care with her hair, too, pulling it back in a tight chignon. Madame Montiard had loaned her eighteen-carat-gold earrings, which theoretically would draw attention to the mark of Margolis on her neck, should anyone be interested in confirming her claim.

André was also dressed conservatively in a dark suit, quite appropriate to a man who aspired to be prime minister. Darned if Nicole didn't think he looked better in jeans.

For all of these preparations and the answers to questions she and André had rehearsed, she was grateful for him at her side, his hand resting protectively at the small of her back. She knew in the crowd around her there were several dark-suited bodyguards André had hired—all of them with guns. She had certainly gotten herself into the middle of some serious court intrigue.

Keeping her smile in place, she took a deep breath before answering about the twentieth question from the gathered reporters.

"I came to Margolis because I have always had a deep affection for the country. Only after I learned of the economic problems and what the people have been suffering did I feel I had to step forward to assist in any way I could."

A flashbulb went off and she blinked.

"Would you care to comment on your hasty marriage?"

André spoke up. "When two people are meant for each other, love happens quickly."

Nicole didn't deny his statement. It was all part of the plan designed to put the current prime minister on the defensive.

"Has Hendrik Meier-Wahl officially welcomed you to the country as yet?" asked a man holding a microphone.

Boy, has he! she thought. With a bang. Keeping her sweet smile in place, she said, "Not as yet. I am looking forward to meeting him, however." And letting him know just what I think of him and his thugs."

"We understand there was an attempt made on your life. Do you have any idea who might want you out of the way?" That from a middle-aged reporter with a cigarette dangling out of his mouth. He'd asked several questions, all of them polite but penetrating.

"We did experience one unfortunate incident," she conceded, intentionally understating the case. "At this point we certainly wouldn't want to make any accusations. The police are investigating." Two of the most bored, disinterested cops she had ever met.

"Are you supporting your husband's try for the prime minister's job?" another reporter asked.

In regal style, she blessed André with her warmest, supportive smile. "I believe André Montiard has the best interests of the country and its people at heart."

He returned her smile, communicating that he agreed with her assessment.

"Your Highness, would that be true if the monarchy were reestablished?"

She shifted her attention to the questioner, a woman wearing heavy makeup and a garish hat with a floppy brim. "I am a firm believer in democracy."

"But if there were a show of support?"

She leveled an icy look at the persistent reporter. "George Washington didn't believe in kings or queens, and that's what I learned in school. I'll leave it at that."

Sensing her frayed nerves, André stepped forward. "Thank you, gentlemen, ladies. That is all of the questions for today. My wife would like an opportunity to take a look around the castle. It is, after all, her ancestral home."

There were a few more shouted questions, but André had her firmly by the arm, escorting her through the gates into the castle.

"Whew. That was tougher than I expected. Did I do all right?" she asked, still nervous about her new, public role, as well as the threat of violence Hendrik represented.

"Wonderfully well. You are such a born politician, Princess, I am glad I am not running for a seat in parliament against you. You will be seen on the evening news in every living room throughout Margolis. And then the world. The people will love you."

"I hope they love me enough so Hendrik doesn't dare try to kill us again."

With an odd sort of awareness, she realized she had enjoyed the press conference, if not the reason she'd come up with the idea. Adrenaline still surged through her veins. In school, she had been the one who stood apart from the crowd, never wanting to be the center of attention. As she and André walked along a path through the castle courtyard, she noted the curious stares of government workers, who were no doubt aware of the hubbub she had created with the media. She suddenly acknowledged that she wanted to *be* someone, someone important.

She wanted to live in a place like the House of Montiard or even in this ancient, sprawling castle. She wanted to shed her past. She wanted, God help her, to love a prince, a man who could handle a crowd of reporters, drink champagne from a crystal glass, and fork hay into a wagon with equal ease. And make her laugh in the process.

André.

The press of tears burned at the back of her eyes. A quirk of fate had given her a chance to taste ambrosia, to let her be queen for a day. Then those same fickle forces would snatch it all away because real people couldn't live their dreams. At least, not for long.

And she hated herself for wanting what she couldn't have.

Together she and André toured the great hall with its incredible display of Medieval long swords, broad-blade axes and chain mail, and visited the chapel, marveling at the dark oak railing stained by the hands of a thousand supplicants. They viewed assorted kitchens, pantries and storerooms. At each step Nicole was aware of André next to her, touching her in subtle seduction—his fingers lightly on her arm one moment, then his forearm draped across her shoulder, and all too often his hand on her waist as he explained the history of a country he loved and she barely knew. She absorbed his lessons, enjoying his deep, sonorous voice, and remembered how his lips tasted, the feel of his body brushing against hers.

They paused in front of an oil painting of King Stanislow that was at least fifteen feet high, a larger-than-life rendition of the monarch in a regal stance, his hounds gathered around him for the hunt. The plaque below the portrait read Stanislow Henri Karl LeDeaux. "Do you see the family resemblance?" André asked.

She cocked her head. "Hmm, it's hard to tell since he's wearing a beard."

"I am eternally grateful that particular characteristic was not passed along to you."

She gave him a teasing jab with her elbow. "The auburn hair is about the same shade, but his eyes are kind of narrow and look quite blue."

"I much prefer yours. Particularly when you are angry, the flakes of gold in your eyes flash like sparks of fire."

A flush of pleasure warmed her cheeks. "That's a rather romantic description, don't you think?"

"I am a very romantic fellow, or had you not noticed?"

"I've noticed you tend to have a one-track mind."

"Only where you are concerned, Princess."

She doubted that. Not with all the women she suspected threw themselves at his feet.

What did surprise her, though, was that she felt little or no connection to the man in the painting. Somehow she had thought she would. She'd already developed an attachment to the rural countryside and the people who lived there, but she felt nothing at all toward the man from whom she'd apparently inherited the mark of Margolis.

She touched the side of her neck. Maybe it was nothing more than a freckle, after all, and the claims she had just touted to the press were a fraud. Wouldn't that leave both her and André in a mess.... He'd only married her because of that mark, she realized. And now he'd put his reputation on the line in front of the entire world by announcing she was the heir.

God help her, for *his* sake she hoped it was true. Or at the very least, she prayed no one would discover she was an impostor. The housekeeper's kid from Beverly Hills who was trying to commit a crime a lot worse than sneaking into the movie theater through the back door.

When they stepped into the queen's bedchamber, Nicole drew a quick, admiring breath. Black lacquer furniture with gold foil rested on a Persian carpet of complimentary colors. The four-poster was set apart from the rest of the room in an alcove draped with gold curtains. Tapestries in subdued pastels created a feeling that everything in the room floated through the clouds, making it look like a scene out of a fairy tale or the Arabian Nights.

"Now this, my princess, is a room made for love." André's smooth, rich voice slid over her flesh like warm gold.

She turned to him. In his dark eyes she saw the depth of both his passion and concern. "You're worried, aren't you?"

He trailed the back of his hand across her cheek. "Though I often play the part, I am not a fool, Nicole. There is great risk in challenging Hendrik. I would never forgive myself if you were injured, or worse."

"After yesterday, I know what I'm getting into. You didn't force me."

His gaze swept across her features, warming her cheeks, then settling on her mouth. "I would never force a woman."

"So you've said." He wasn't coercing her now. In fact, she was the one lifting her face, straining toward him, wanting the feel of his lips on hers. Perhaps it was the excitement of the day or the peril she faced that made her feel reckless. Or perhaps it was his compelling eyes or his provocative masculine scent that muddled her reason. But here, in a room made for fantasies, she wanted to kiss André Montiard.

"I would urge caution on you." His hand slid to the column of her neck and she felt her pulse throb against his palm.

"I'll consider myself forewarned." Though his warning was no louder in her mind than the clear, pure sound of a delicate silver bell ringing in the distance.

He lowered his head toward hers. "Princess..." His husky plea rasped against every one of her nerve endings.

The first brush of his lips was as delicate as spun glass, weaving lustrous sensations around her. Iridescent warmth filled her body, pulsing with liquid color. Subdued golds and yellows took on a fiery quality. The black she had seen in his eyes echoed in her mind as polished onyx. Extraordinarily bright. Reflecting her own needs that had long gone unmet.

When his fingers slid along her neck and plowed their way into her coiled hair, her hands sought the same kind of sensuous pleasure. She ran her palms up the smooth fabric of his jacket, then to his wide shoulders, and finally to that spot where she could caress the chocolate-brown hair that curled at his collar. Luxurious strands entwined her fingers. She trembled, drew a sharp breath, and he deepened the kiss.

His tongue glazed across sensitive, innocent flesh. Exploring. Testing. A part of her seemed to fracture into a thousand brilliant lights, like sunlight pouring across a diamond or slicing through cut glass.

Like a skilled craftsman, he added layer after layer of sensation to the simple experience of a kiss. She felt dizzy with the need to study every nuance of his technique in exquisite detail. To learn and, like an apprentice, demonstrate her newfound knowledge.

When Nicole's tongue met his in a tentative thrust, André's body responded with a spiraling tightness that jolted him almost painfully. No kiss had ever affected him with such power, no woman had ever tasted so sweet. Hunger for more and a desire to maintain some semblance of control warred within him. Though this bedchamber was a room perfectly suited for love, and for Nicole, it was also a public place.

Unable to resist testing his control, he cupped her buttocks, pulling her against his thighs where he pressed his arousal against her softness. She moaned a throaty sound and he crossed her lips again in a kiss that molded their mouths together with melting passion.

"It seems the young lovers have chosen to claim the bedchamber before they claim the throne."

The commanding voice cut through the quiet, breathy silence of the room.

Cursing under his breath, André turned. "Hendrik."

Chapter Seven

Stunned. Disoriented. Her body still pulsating from André's kiss, Nicole could hardly catch her breath. Nor could she reconcile the distinguished gray-haired gentleman standing at the entrance to the queen's bedchamber with the man André had told her about.

A villainous tyrant?

While his eyes might be considered slightly cold, Hendrik was tall and slender, with a thoroughly political smile, which he bestowed on Nicole.

In fact, except for a rich European accent, Hendrik could have passed for the CEO of any company in America. In a way, that made him even more frightening.

André looped his arm protectively around her back, his hand cupping the curve of her shoulder. "What do you want, Hendrik?"

"Why, only to welcome the Princess home, of course," he said with smooth European charm. "It seems I have been lax in expressing our country's hospitality. But then, you appear to have made her feel more than welcome.''

"At least he didn't try to drop a pipe bomb in my lap," she said.

Hendrik lifted his eyebrows with a fair amount of disdain. "I understand there was some unpleasantness at Jean Paul's farm yesterday."

"I'll bet you understand," André accused. "I know I am fair game for your assassination attempts, but you have stooped to a new low when you involve more innocent people. My brother's family—"

"I tire of your slanderous remarks, Montiard, all of them politically motivated. Perhaps your sweet young bride would be interested to learn *you* were the one responsible for your brother's death."

André's body went rigid; his fingers flexed into her flesh. "You lying bastard!" he swore.

"Easy, André," she warned. "The way to get back at Hendrik is to beat his socks off at the polls."

Smirking, Hendrik said, "Your wife is quite right, *monsieur.* Not that I believe it is possible."

At that moment two burly men appeared at the entrance to the queen's bedchamber. Fear constricted Nicole's throat. They were Hendrik's thugs, and André's hired guards were nowhere in sight. Surely Hendrik wouldn't try anything in the castle, not with the press probably still roaming around outside.

"Do not get too complacent, Meier-Wahl," André warned tightly. "The people are on to you."

With an easy shrug, Hendrik said, "You do not have the votes to beat me. Your people will be most fortunate to claim victory in a half dozen districts. That you might gain enough to hold a majority of the house seats stretches the imagination beyond belief."

"We will win if it is an honest election."

One side of Hendrik's lips curled into a sly smile. "Why would someone of my experience permit that?" He laughed, an evil sound, then reached for Nicole's hand. Bowing, he brushed his moist lips across the back of her fingers. She shivered with barely concealed revulsion. "I only regret that not all of my plans have been as successful as my reelection will be."

She snatched her hand back, counting her blessings it had been André, not Hendrik, who had kidnapped her. "Fixing the election isn't going to work this time, *Mister* Meier-Wahl. The whole world will be watching."

"If you really think an upstart political novice can beat me, then you are even more naive than Montiard and his Labor party associates, my dear."

Lifting her chin stubbornly, she slid her arm around André's waist. "We'll just wait and see." As a kid, she had been easily intimidated by men as powerful as Hendrik. This time, she wasn't going to back down. Besides, André was worth about ten Hendriks.

He cocked her an amused smile. "As you wish." With another slight bow, he left the room, trailed by his overmuscled thugs, rather like Madame Montiard's dogs followed after her.

Nicole blew out a sigh.

At the same time, André uncurled fingers that had balled into fists. A muscle rippled at his jaw. "Some days I think we would all be better off if I simply strangled him."

"You don't mean that," Nicole said, her voice soothing across the rough edges of his anger. "There isn't a murderous bone in your body."

"No? There are those who would believe otherwise."

She frowned. "What do you mean?"

"Nothing," he said roughly, knowing the guilty sores that Hendrik had opened were still too painful to probe. "It is time we leave. For the moment, we have worn out our welcome at Castle Margolis."

NICOLE WAS still recalling her unpleasant encounter with Hendrik the next morning as the gaggle of dachshunds nipped at her heels. At least the memory, combined with the rambunctious dogs, distracted her from thoughts of the kiss she had shared with André. A subject very much on her mind, one that had kept her awake a good part of the night. The way André had cut off her questions also troubled her, though not nearly as much as her own yearning to enjoy more of his deep, hungry kisses.

Foolish woman, she admonished herself.

He might be encouraging her to play the role of heir apparent for his own political purposes, but that didn't mean he expected her to hang around after the election. Men like André weren't into commitment, as her mother had discovered.

"Mimi! Edgar! Do leave poor Nicole alone." Madame Montiard swept into the room wearing a velvet morning robe and making a valiant effort to herd the dogs away from Nicole's feet.

"It's all right, *madame*. I think I may even be getting used to them."

"They are a pesky lot, I admit." Seating herself at the head of the elegant rosewood dining table inlaid with an elaborate design in pear wood and sycamore, Madame Montiard waved her hand, signaling breakfast could be served. "But the little creatures keep me company."

"I'm sure they do," Nicole agreed. Sunlight poured through the French doors into the family dining room, promising another hot summer day.

Katja appeared from the kitchen with a great tray filled with plates of sweet rolls, toast, eggs and sausages, enough food to feed the entire town of San Margo. The delicious smells wafting into the room with the maid's arrival made Nicole's stomach rumble.

"Where is that grandson of mine? Doesn't he know breakfast is ready?"

"I am sorry, *madame*." The maid dipped a curtsy. "He came into the kitchen quite early this morning, had a bit of coffee and a sweet, then left. He seemed in a hurry to get to work on his cars."

"Well, never mind." She waved off the girl. "I did want to talk with you both about the party," she said to Nicole, "but you will do quite nicely, I am sure."

Nicole selected a piece of wheat toast and scooped a helping of eggs onto her plate. "I'd be happy to help in any way I can."

"Do have some of that spicy peach marmalade on your toast, dear. Cook's own secret recipe, I am told." Madame Montiard helped herself to a roll, plus scrambled eggs. "I have been trying to decide whether we ought to have one musical group, or two."

"Two? For a small party, that seems a bit extravagant."

"I suppose so. But you young people prefer much different music than we old folks enjoy. I was thinking about putting a small band—only five or six pieces—out by the garden. Perhaps one of those British groups?" She shimmied her narrow shoulders in an odd imitation of rock 'n roll. "Something really hot?"

Nicole nearly choked on her toast. "Don't do that on my account. I'd really like to keep this whole affair rather low key." Particularly since no one except Madame Montiard expected this marriage to last more than a couple of months. Madame Montiard, and the Gypsy fortune-teller, Nicole reminded herself.

"Naturally, dear. Whatever you would like, I quite understand. Still, it would be nice..."

Shifting the subject, Nicole said, "Tell me, Madame Montiard, how close were André and his brother?" If she couldn't get answers from André, maybe his grandmother could fill in the blanks.

"Ah, as boys they were like two peas in a pod." She held two fingers together, symbolizing the close relationship. "My son—their father—had little time for them after their mother left."

"Left? You mean, she deserted her children?"

"Regretfully, my son was not an easy man for a woman to live with. I saw it coming but was helpless to change things. And she, his first wife, was full of pride. The others—" She shrugged. "They did not care so much as long as there was money for them to spend. Bushels of it. When he tired of them, he simply sent them away. With a good many francs in their pockets, of course."

"But André's mother...to leave her own children... That must have hurt the boys terribly." Even though Nicole's relationship with her mother hadn't been perfect, she could imagine the sense of loss growing up without her would have meant.

"I do not think André has forgiven her yet, in spite of the fact she was not entirely to blame. And she did try, poor child." The older woman broke a piece of sausage in two to give to the dogs, and there was a great deal of scurrying around as they competed for the tidbit. "But that was not the real tragedy that drove a wedge between the boys. That was Monique."

"A woman?"

"A pretty little thing. She lived in the village, and her father was a minor official in the government. Customs, I believe. Nothing important. In many ways, because of her background and lack of training, Monique was not suited to this life. It is not always as easy at it appears, as I am sure you know. But André fell in love. In matters of the heart, often we cannot choose, and he was quite young." Madame Montiard scolded her dogs for some new infraction of the rules, then went on with her story. "Unfortunately, Monique could not, or would not, return André's affection. Instead she became enamored of Christian, pursuing him until he relented. Poor André... I believe that changed him. For the sake of his brother, he tried not to let his feelings show, but I noticed the difference."

"How? What did he do?" Feeling a wave of sympathy for André, Nicole studied his grandmother over the rim of her coffee cup.

"He became very carefree. With the women, you know?" She shrugged as though such behavior was to be expected. "And other times he would hide himself away with his cars, losing himself for hours in his garage, giving those smelly machines the love he should have been giving to a woman.''

Until now, Nicole hadn't considered André as a tragic figure. Perhaps she had misjudged him. With his cocky grin, he didn't seem the kind of man who had experienced a whole lot of heartbreak in his life. But maybe his easy smile was as fraudulent as her claim to the throne.

Katja interrupted Nicole's thoughts by appearing at the swinging door again, dipping her usual curtsies. ''Excuse me, *madame*, but Monsieur André's machine is beeping in his office. Should I call him in from the garage?''

''What machine?'' Nicole asked.

''Oh, that dreadful facsimile thing. A modern slave-driver. Always going off at the most inconvenient times. It carries on till you push a button or something. I really don't understand how—''

''I'll take care of it.'' Nicole shoved back her chair on the hardwood floor. Dealing with a machine would give her a moment to consider what she had just learned. Perhaps there was more depth to André than she had guessed. Clearly he had been badly hurt by *two* women in his life. Little wonder he viewed relationships as fleeting, and women as less than trustworthy.

A mirror image of her own feelings toward men, she mused.

By the time she'd figured out the intricacies of the facsimile machine, and received the message, the

beeper announced another was waiting. Fast on the
heels of the second came another, and then a fourth.
Without even thinking, she glanced at each one as it
came through.

"Wow," she said after perusing each of the fac-
similied newspaper articles. Her press conference had
generated quite a bit of interest. If her antique store
failed, she'd have to consider PR for a career.

Smiling broadly, she scooped up the papers and
went in search of André. "Watch out, Hendrik," she
said out loud. "We've got you on the run now."

As EXPECTED, she found André in the garage. Or
more accurately, she spotted two feet and a pair of
overall-clad legs sticking out from beneath his Ferrari. A chest-high toolbox stood open near the front
of the car, and there were assorted wrenches and
screwdrivers strewn on the concrete floor.

"Hello under there," she called.

He grunted a muffled "Good morning."

"What are you doing?"

"Changing the oil. Be right with you."

"You got a bunch of facsimilies I thought you'd
want to see. We made quite a splash in the international press yesterday."

"We did?" He dollied himself out from under the
car. The moment Nicole saw his grease-spattered
face, with his wayward lock of hair drooping across
his forehead, she felt a surge of emotion very much
like love. For all of his cocky good looks, André had

suffered heartbreak. Her fingers flexed with the forbidden desire to smooth away that persistent curl and feel again the luxurious strands of his hair running through her fingers. A heated sensation coiled through her, thrumming low in her body. Her heartbeat throbbed an irregular cadence.

From his vantage point, André relished the improbable moment. Nicole was looking down at him with undisguised desire. Her eyes were wide, her lips parted. She had once mentioned she had a yearning for auto mechanics. André was certainly that, with his overalls covered with grease, and probably his face, as well. If he had set out to seduce a woman, he would not have chosen a garage for a romantic setting, nor would he have arrived with his hands coated with oil.

Yet she was responding to him. The signs were all there. Even the rapid rise and fall of her breasts. Just thinking about how their weight would feel in his hands made him hard.

Afraid to break the spell of this sweet, torturous moment, André allowed himself the exquisite pleasure of studying the shapely length of Nicole's legs. They rose in perfect unison from sandaled feet, ever upward, finally escaping just below the vee of her thighs to hide in a pair of bright yellow shorts. Her flesh was smooth, glowing warmly with a California tan. He wondered if her swimsuit had left a pale line and what the flesh that had never been kissed by the sun would look like. And taste like. Or if her skin would feel as silken as it appeared, as soft and smooth as a baby's. And if the curls covering her womanhood would be the same vibrant shade as the hair she wore in a loose braid that hung down her back.

He had a thousand questions, all of them erotic, each of them unanswered except that kissing Nicole was like tasting a bit of heaven. Sleeping in an adjacent room with locked doors between them was closer to purgatory.

He stood and used a cloth to clean oil from his hands. "What are the papers saying?" He knew what her eyes had communicated. He intended to explore the message in as much detail as possible, as soon as possible.

She blinked, visibly drawing back into herself, and he felt a sense of lost opportunity.

"They've dubbed me Princess Nicole, to no one's surprise." Her voice was slightly breathless, suggesting she wasn't yet as fully under control as she would want André to believe. "There's lots of speculation about the upcoming election and your rivalry with Hendrik, and how my arrival will affect all that. I think there'd be a real stink if either of us had an unexplained accident about now."

"That is what we had hoped." He took the stack of papers from her, held her anxious gaze for an instant, then read quickly through the headlines. Returning Princess To Help Husband's Election, Lost Heir Appears, Princess Reclaims Heritage. A small article drew his particular attention: Monarchists To Organize.

"I do not like the sounds of this one," he said, frowning.

"What's that?" She peered over his shoulder, close enough so her breast brushed against his arm. His groin muscles instinctively tightened in response.

With an act of will, he ignored the sensations she inspired. "It looks as if some dissidents who are unhappy with the current political parties are hoping to reestablish a monarchy."

"But that's ridiculous. Margolis has been a democracy since World War I."

She took a hasty step back. He wondered if she knew what her touch had done to him. Or if she had actually intended that light brush? Based on his experience, women were perfectly capable of their own form of seduction. "It would not be such an impossible idea," he said, observing her reactions closely. She looked so damn innocent, and still he was suspicious. "Now that they have you to carry their banner."

"I made it perfectly clear at the press conference I didn't want to be queen of anything."

"Sometimes people hear only what they want to hear," André mused. And they imagined the rest. It would be easy for a young, naive woman to get caught up in the excitement of pomp and circumstance without understanding the full responsibilities.

"Then I will simply have to say it again. You're the one who should lead this country. Not me. Besides . . ." She looked up at him, her gaze steady, her hazel eyes questioning. "After the election, I'm going back home. To open my antique shop."

The painful reminder twisted with a shout of denial through André's gut. "Yes, that is what we have agreed."

He saw a flash of something in her eyes. Pain? Disappointment? But she turned away so quickly he couldn't be sure. Perhaps he was the one imagining things, like passion and desire. For him, the sensations were quite real, fisting and straining through his body. There had been a brief moment there when if she had asked him to throw away all of the Montiard wealth and become a mechanic in some grubby garage in the States, he would have willingly, foolishly agreed. To see that hungry look in her eyes every day would have been worth the price.

But women—and passion—did not last that long. Of that, the Montiard men had learned their lessons well.

THE FIRST CONTINGENT arrived that afternoon. *Monarchists.*

Flustered, Nicole whispered, "What am I supposed to say?"

"Whatever you like, Princess," André replied, looking so complacent she wanted to scream.

She fumed. Why didn't these people understand? As an American, she couldn't possibly buy into a monarchy. Sure, as a kid she might have pranced around in the privacy of her own room using an old blanket for a robe and a bit of cut-out cardboard for a crown. But this was grown-up stuff. She didn't care who her ancestor was. She didn't belong here, not among all these fine things in the House of Montiard. Certainly not taking up residence in a drafty old castle, however lovely the furnishings, whatever her fantasies might be. She was no longer a child filled with wishful dreams. She wasn't a queen, and never would be. She had to remember that.

"You're the politician," she reminded him from between clenched teeth. "Think of a way to get them on your side, for heaven's sake."

"You are the best leverage I have. As they say in your country, go for it."

She rolled her eyes.

Fortunately, when the visitors had been announced, she'd changed into a simple skirt and blouse, one of her traveling outfits. It was hardly regal, but better than her shorts and the tank top she'd worn that morning. Even dressed in a sport shirt and slacks, André looked far more impressive than she.

As she entered the main salon with its marble floors and alabaster columns, every one of the dozen guests made a low bow or curtsy. Dressed in their finest, though not necessarily fashionable clothes, most of the visitors were well up in years, far too old to be showing her such deference.

"Your Majesty," they mumbled in unison.

"Please, call me Nicole," she said as she shook hands with the first man who stepped forward. She certainly didn't feel comfortable being called Madame Montiard. That honor belonged to André's grandmother. And the title of Mrs. Montiard felt entirely too fraudulent.

"We are grateful for this audience, Your Majesty. I am Vilhelm Seville. My grandfather had the privilege of serving King Stanislow and was present when he died at the hands of his enemies." This gentleman was younger than the rest, about forty, with thinning hair and sallow skin. "It will be my honor to serve you when you reclaim the throne."

"As I explained to the press, Mr. Seville, I have no intention of becoming queen. My husband, André—"

"Please hear us out, Your Highness," a frail, stooped woman said. She pressed an old photo into Nicole's hand, a picture of a girl about ten standing next to an imposing figure of a man. "I knew King Stanislow personally. I was only a child, of course, but he was a fine gentleman. So kind. Our country was sound then. And now..." She looked at Nicole with watery eyes. "Please, you must help us."

And so the stories went. Each visitor had some personal connection to the monarchy, and all of them hoped Nicole's return would mean an improvement in their lives. Both embarrassed and flattered by their attention, Nicole caught André's eye. In answer to her unspoken plea, he simply smiled. Lord, she wished he'd toss her a life preserver. She was definitely in over her head with these people.

Finally sensing her discomfort, André stepped up beside Nicole and slipped his arm around her waist in a reassuring gesture. He had never imagined feeling such pride in the woman he married. Not only was she beautiful, she handled herself with considerable aplomb under most difficult circumstances . . . as though she were born to the throne, he mused.

The leader of the Monarchist party disturbed him, however. By tapping into nostalgia, the man and his followers were likely to have significant appeal among the voters. André did not like to think about splitting the vote among those who opposed Hendrik. Gaining a majority of the members in the House of Commons was critical to André's plans.

"We have begun circulating a petition," Vilhelm Seville informed her. "Our hope is that the people of Margolis will have a chance to vote in favor of the restoration of the throne."

"I wish you wouldn't do that," she insisted.

"We understand your reluctance, Your Majesty. But if it is the people's will, surely you would not refuse your duty."

Nicole stared at the man in disbelief. Duty? Her obligation was to help André become prime minister, not take his place as ruler of the country, a task she wasn't at all prepared to handle.

By the time the entourage of supporters left, Nicole felt drained. The entire country suffered from selective hearing.

"What am I going to do?" she asked André. "They absolutely refused to listen to what I was saying."

"Perhaps you did not completely believe it yourself."

She felt the heat of guilt color her cheeks. "What do you mean by that?"

"You like the attention. Being a princess has its advantages. Certainly, you would not be the first woman to be lured by the trappings of wealth."

"That's not so." At least, she resisted the temptation she knew was her weakness. "My sole concern is to help you."

"We shall see."

"Do you think I don't know my place?" she asked, an emptiness filling her chest. *Her place* didn't include being a part of André's life, or his wealth.

"I only think the monarchists will not give up their cause so easily. And you, my dear, would fill their need as a standard bearer."

With a shake of her head, she denied the possibility even as she admitted to herself the temptation would be difficult to resist.

ANDRÉ'S WORDS were still troubling Nicole that Saturday night as she prepared for the wedding party in their honor. He'd been so busy since the monarchists' visit they'd had little time to talk. And as surely as though she had become addicted, she missed his bantering, his cocky grin, and the way he made her feel so thoroughly feminine. Without her realizing quite when it had happened, she was hooked on André Montiard.

Worry scoring her forehead, she studied her reflection in the vanity mirror while Katja did something quite exquisite with her hair, piling it on top of her head in a vast array of ringlets and curls.

"You're incredible, Katja. If you ever decide to go to America you could make a fortune as a hairdresser for the stars."

The girl blushed sweetly. "Your hair is so lovely, Princess, it is easy to make it do lovely things." She rolled another thick strand around the curling iron and held it for a moment, testing it with her fingers. "I have a question I wish to ask, but I am afraid my words will make you angry."

"Ask anything you'd like, Katja." Nicole smiled into the mirror.

"It is this strange custom of you Americans, to put a lock on the door between a man and his wife. I do not think my Pierre would like such a thing. Even now, when we are not yet married..." The girl's voice trailed off into an embarrassed silence.

"What makes you think it's an American custom?"

"*Monsieur* said it was so. When you first came to the House of Montiard we all thought it quite strange. But he said it is a way to make a husband most eager to be with his wife." She giggled. "I do not think my Pierre could be any more eager than he already is."

"I'm sure that's true." But the lock had been intended to *discourage* the man, not the reverse. Perhaps André had made up the story to save face.

"I know this custom is working for you. I see *monsieur*'s eyes follow you with much hunger."

"You do?"

"Oh, yes. Sometimes when you are not watching, I know such a small thing as a lock would not stop *monsieur*. It must be very exciting when he comes to you so eager."

"Yes, well . . ." Actually, André had been the picture of restraint lately. Nicole suspected the barrier she'd erected with the lock was making *her* eager, not the other way around. Something about reverse psychology, she imagined.

And what would it matter, she wondered suddenly, if she unbolted the door? They were married, after all. Granted the arrangement was temporary. But other women made love with men they barely knew. In the past she'd been accused of attaching too much importance to sex. Perhaps it was time to set such prudery aside.

No! The word almost came out as a painful cry.

With an awful spiral of self-awareness, she knew she couldn't be casual about making love. Not with any man, and certainly not with André.

Far better to keep the locks in place, she told herself sternly. Then she would be able to return home with her heart intact. *Home*—a tiny apartment and storefront shop that had yet to materialize. Hardly the stuff of which dreams were made.

"There," Katja announced, satisfied with her efforts. "Now for the dress."

Nicole stood while the maid lifted the diaphanous silk gown over her head. In contrast to the simple dress Nicole had selected at the ready-to-wear store, this designer garment André had ordered bespoke quiet elegance. In a rich shade of gold that enhanced her auburn hair, the fabric clung to her bodice in a lacy insert and hugged her hips before flaring into a graceful skirt that reached to her ankles. The long, sheer sleeves were more revealing than modest, and the scalloped neckline suggested rather than disclosed. A gown fit for a queen.

A reflected movement in the mirror caught her eye. As he had that first night, André was standing at the open French doors, devastatingly handsome in his tux. His lips canted into an arrogant, cocky smile, and his eyes bore with dark passion into her back.

"Good evening, Princess," he said in a voice that was low and raspy, unfairly intimate in a room that suddenly felt too small to enclose all of the emotions that had been warring within Nicole's mind.

In that instant all of her newfound resolve liquified like fine glass melting in a fiery furnace. Tonight there would be no locks on her door.

Chapter Eight

"That will be all, Katja," André said, entering the room in a lazy, arrogant stroll.

Turning, the maid gasped. "But, *monsieur,* I need to finish dressing—"

"Allow me the pleasure."

Every inch of Nicole's flesh flamed under his dark-eyed scrutiny, even skin that was modestly hidden beneath the silk of her dress. Her heart did quite an amazing imitation of a kettle drum, and her breath lodged in her throat.

Devastatingly handsome became an understatement suited for mere mortals. André was a god, a sculpture in black and white, with a slash of scarlet cummerbund drawing attention to his hard, flat stomach. Distantly aware Katja had left the room, Nicole watched his approach in the mirror. Power. Vitality. Sheer masculinity. All of those words described him. And as he came closer, she caught his musky male scent mixing with his leathery cologne.

Her body reacted with a tight clenching deep between her thighs.

"May I?" he asked softly, although it wasn't really a question. He would have his way, of that Nicole was quite certain from the determined glint in his dark eyes.

His fingers deftly—seductively—worked her zipper up her back, from her waist to that sensitive hollow between her shoulder blades. His hands paused there, touching her, heating her skin, teasing her imagination, before he completed the simple task.

With a dip of his head, he placed a soft, warm kiss on her flesh at the juncture of her neck and shoulder. She shuddered, feeling the heat of his lips coil through her, absorbing and melting her essence in a single, fiery caress.

"André?" she whispered.

"You look lovely." His husky praise poured over her like warm honey, sweet and tempting. "And now for the finishing touch."

From his inside jacket pocket he retrieved a narrow velvet box. He flipped open the lid. A blinding array of diamonds glistened in the reflected light.

With exquisite care, he lifted the necklace—so wide it was almost a collar—from the box and placed it around Nicole's neck. Interspersed with the diamonds, four large emeralds sparkled with their own extravagant radiance.

"They're real." She sighed in awe. She'd never seen, never imagined, any jewels more elegant.

"Of course. These gems have been in the Montiard family for more than one hundred years." One corner of his mouth curled into an approving smile. "And they have never looked better on any woman, Princess. As I had hoped, the emeralds make your eyes look almost green."

"Really?" She'd always thought of her eyes as quite ordinary. Until now.

He gazed at her in the mirror as his knuckles skimmed along her neck. "Or perhaps it is something else you are feeling that makes the color darken?"

"No, I..." She swallowed the lie. She knew what he was seeing in her eyes. Undisguised passion. Valiantly she tried to remember all of the reasons she shouldn't make love with André Montiard; not a single one came to mind.

"The guests have begun to arrive. We will have to go downstairs soon."

"Yes."

"Regretfully." His heated breath warmed her cheek and the vibrations of his husky voice swirled through her senses.

"Yes," she repeated. Wavering under the spell he created, she leaned back, bringing her body into shockingly intimate contact with the strength of his. His unyielding chest, his flat stomach, the hard evidence of his arousal.

His arms encircled her, strong and dark against the pale gold of her dress. "This is one time when I shall hope the guests depart as promptly as they have arrived.''

She knew what he was saying, what he wanted after the party, their wedding celebration. The knowledge shivered through her like fine wine. Refusal teased at the tip of her tongue, then vanished with every other resolve she had made.

''Say the word, Princess.'' His teeth nibbled at the ridge of her ear, a tender bite that sent a spasm of air through her lungs. ''I need to know you want me as much as I want you.''

''Yes.'' The quiet admission came easily from her heart.

His eyes closed a moment and his arms tightened around her in an elegant statement of self-restraint. ''Good.''

She carried the promise of his words with her as she took his arm and he escorted her to the curving stairway that led to the main salon. The crystal chandelier hanging from the domed ceiling sparkled almost as brightly as the necklace she wore.

The voices of mingling guests hushed as she and André began their descent of the stairway into the crowd. Every eye looked upward. Though she took a deep breath and forced a smile, their faces were a blur. All she could think about was André. How he would undress her, how his dark hands would cover her body, and how she would permit him the ultimate in intimacy. That final moment rose up in her imagination with startling clarity while he introduced her to each bowing guest. She pictured herself lying in André's arms upstairs in her bedroom, the draped curtains pulled around them, and thought about his gentleness. She was consumed by the sweet agony of anticipation.

She accepted a glass of champagne from a passing waiter but knew she was already intoxicated with more than mere alcohol.

The crowd ebbed and flowed around her. Clearly Madame Montiard's definition of a *small* party differed from Nicole's by several hundred people. Occasionally she caught a glimpse of one of the men she knew André had hired as a guard. They looked only slightly less dangerous in tuxedos than they did in their street clothes. Surely nothing bad would happen to disrupt the party with them around.

"You remember the persistent reporter at our press conference," André said, introducing her to Robert von Helman.

"Yes, of course." With her smile carefully in place, Nicole extended her hand. What she remembered of that day was André's kiss in the queen's bedchamber, the exquisite, shattering feeling of his lips on hers. She eagerly looked forward to a repeat of the same heart-stopping experience. "Are you here as a reporter or a friend, Mr. von Helman?"

Pulling his dangling cigarette from his mouth long enough to brush a kiss to the back of her hand, Robert said, "Both, Your Highness. It is the way of the press. We tuck every tidbit we learn to the back of our minds, then . . ." His thin lips slid into an engaging smile. "Perhaps, if we are very fortunate, the information reappears again when we need it."

"In that case, I'll try not to do anything that would prove embarrassing in print." Like asking André to take her back upstairs this very minute, forgetting his friends, and finally doing exactly what he had wanted her to do since the very first moment he'd dragged her from the cathedral steps.

"Robert has contacts all over the world," André explained, "as well as a photographic memory. He keeps us all on our toes."

Robert acknowledged the praise with a nod. "As a matter of fact, I have made some progress in that matter we discussed."

Nicole's attention slid from the reporter to André's questioning eyebrow and back again.

"One of my associates in Paris has managed to track Nicolas LeDeaux as far as that city. Apparently that is where he fled just before the war broke out and his father's subsequent assassination."

"That is good news, Robert."

"Nicolas was King Stanislow's son. Have you two been trying to check my story?" Nicole asked, frowning.

A gentle squeeze of André's hand at her waist reassured her. "Robert is simply being a thorough reporter."

"The trail after Paris seems to have grown cold," Robert said. "As yet, my associates in the States have been unable to confirm immigration records. But given the hectic nature of those times, I do not find that usual.''

Nicole added a feeling of unease to go with her heightened sense of sexual awareness. Playing the role of heir to the throne was supposed to *help* André. If von Helman found information that disproved her claim, it could be damaging to his campaign. No one would believe she had innocently accepted her grandmother's story as being fact.

And Nicole wanted to do more than simply help André. She wanted to be at his side, a companion and partner in every way. She wanted . . .

She glanced up and their eyes met. His promise was still in the onyx depths, hot and insistent, and she forgot about everything beyond what would happen when the party was finally over.

Still in a daze, she was pulled away to meet other guests, most of whom fussed over her, accepting her claim to the throne without blinking an eye. A part of her enjoyed the attention. She couldn't deny that. But at a more basic, primal level, André was the central focus of her attention. Smoothly sophisticated, his hand touched her in familiar communication—on her back, resting on her shoulder, a caress of her hair—as though they had been lovers for years. She felt oddly breathless, her breasts weighted with longing. The bass sounds of the musical groups vibrated low in her body.

She sipped at her champagne in an effort to cool her parched throat. The result, however, was a increasingly euphoric sensation she couldn't entirely blame on the drink.

On the dance floor, couples swirled around her, the women's skirts shifting in soft, sibilant whispers, their perfumes wafting sweetly through the air. The men spoke in deep, cultured tones. But the only sounds she could hear were André's voice, mesmerizing her, and the sound of her pounding heart.

A jarring, discordant note brought her sharply back to reality as a sexy, platinum blonde approached. From the provocative sway of the woman's hips to her plastic smile, Nicole immediately recognized her as a rival.

The stranger stood on tiptoe to give André a kiss that was both familiar and seductive as hell.

Nicole fumed. She fought the urge to tear the woman's hair out, every long, bleached strand. Definitely poor form in front of all these people. But, boy, if she ever got this sexpot alone . . .

To his credit, André's color deepened as he introduced Marlene Marquette. "An old friend, my brother's former sister-in-law," he explained. "Also, Hendrik's press secretary, which we must not hold against her."

"My congratulations," Marlene said, slicing Nicole a blue-eyed look that would have cut through steel. "Or should I say 'condolences'? Montiard men are not exactly noted for how faithful they are to their wives." She shot André an equally cool look, except her smile was far more genuine. "Or to their girlfriends."

"Pull in your claws, my dear. Nicole is not your enemy."

The young woman raised perfectly arched eyebrows. "No? You underestimate me, my love. I know exactly who is my enemy." She gave Nicole another scathing look. "And it is not a masquerading peasant who is trying to rise above herself."

Oozing sex appeal, along with blatant aggression, Marlene slinked away.

Nicole relaxed jaws that had been clenched together in jealous fury. "That woman hates me." She didn't even want to deal with how much of the truth the woman had intuited—that Nicole was a fraud.

"She is harmless, Princess. A greedy, envious woman. Nothing more."

"But you knew her rather...intimately?"

He shrugged. "Would you question all of my liaisons since I was but a young man?"

No, she wouldn't do that. No wife, certainly not a temporary one, had a right to ask too many questions. But she hated that she cared so much he had a past beyond her knowledge. Or that he had yet to suggest their relationship would last beyond the election.

At André's urging, she turned to meet the next party guest, a narrow-faced man with hair very much the color of straw and just as straight.

"This, my dear, is the man who is responsible for our rather hasty marriage," André announced with a big grin. "May I present Sebastian Ulman, my best friend."

"Are you Jean Paul's son?" Until recently, Nicole would have wanted to punch the lights out of the guy who had gotten her into this mess. Now she was tempted to kiss him.

"Indeed I am, Princess," he said, bowing gallantly over her extended hand, a gesture that caused his hair to swoop across his forehead like a pendulum. Unconsciously, he finger-combed it back in place.

"I've been worried about your mother and father ever since the explosion. Are they all right?"

"Still a bit shaken, but comfortable staying with my sister and her family while the house is repaired. At André's expense, I might add. They both speak very highly of you."

"They're charming. They made me feel right at home."

"Sebastian is my campaign manager...when I can keep him out of the beer halls all night."

He feigned shock at the accusation. "But that is where I do my best work."

"At my expense."

"Naturally."

André laughed. "So? How is the election going?"

"Ah, you are gaining ground by the moment, thanks to your beautiful wife." He nodded to Nicole as he gave her the credit. "Her popularity is growing rapidly and is exceeding all of my expectations. It is my considered opinion you will be dragged into office on her coat—ah, skirt tails."

"There, you see? My marriage to Nicole was a brilliant political decision."

She flushed, both flattered and annoyed by the reminder of her role in her husband's life. "André is perfectly capable of winning without me. He's intelligent, eager to improve the economy, and he cares about the people, certainly more than Hendrik does. André doesn't need me." Although, increasingly, Nicole was beginning to think she needed him.

Sebastian raised his eyebrows. "My God, André. What have you done to this poor, defenseless woman? She actually sounds as though she *likes* you."

"Shut up, friend." André slid his arm around Nicole's waist and gave her an affectionate hug. "If you do not behave yourself, I will see to it your beer ration is revoked."

He rolled his eyes. "In that case, my friend, I shall strive to be on my best behavior."

"See that you do." As much as André enjoyed joking with his friend, the party was dragging so slowly he was considering announcing a fire had broken out in the kitchen. Then everyone would have to leave. Immediately.

He glanced one more time at his Rolex. How many more minutes, or hours, would he have to wait until he could hold Nicole in his arms? He wanted to see her creamy flesh, all of it, and taste the flavor of her full breasts. He wanted to explore her delectable softness, hear her moan into his mouth, and sheath himself in her sweet velvet warmth.

In the midst of all these people, he could only imagine what lay in store for them later. Not too much later, he hoped, the persistent ache in his groin a painful reminder of how long he had already waited.

Geoffrey Landau, a dottering but wealthy old fool and a campaign contributor, made off with Nicole for a dance. André could hardly object. But he missed having her in his arms. Tonight he would take her hard and fast, and then . . .

He smiled in anticipation. They would pleasure each other until long past dawn.

NICOLE HAD NEVER felt so alive, or so filled with trepidation, as they bid the last of the guests goodnight.

Servants scurried around the salons cleaning up the debris, retrieving champagne glasses, wiping up spills and emptying ashtrays. The musicians had long since gone. Madame Montiard had escaped to her private wing hours ago.

"Maybe I should help," she suggested, her fingers fiddling self-consciously with the diamond and emerald necklace at her throat. "The place is such a mess, it will take them forever to straighten things out."

"That is what we pay them for," André pointed out.

"But it's such a big job." And her erotic thoughts had been playing havoc with her imagination all night. Now that the moment of truth had come, panic threatened.

"Surely you have not forgotten our earlier conversation, Princess." He looked her up and down in a slow perusal that left her all the more breathless by its casual claim of ownership. "If so, allow me to remind you."

Tugging her into a secluded alcove beneath the stairs, he caught her mouth in a hungry, demanding kiss. Like a fine piece of furniture can eclipse everything else in a room, André dominated Nicole with his sensuous onslaught. The crushing feel of his mouth was both frightening and thrilling at the same time. The way his hand cupped her buttocks, kneading them, forcing her into the nest of his hips, caused a riot of senations. Wild, primitive forces built within her, feelings she didn't know how to handle, or where they would lead.

With his free hand he massaged one aching, heavy breast. Through the sheer fabric of her dress she felt the warm roughness of his hand with such shocking intimacy it was as though she wore nothing at all. His plunging tongue and the shifting press of his lips moved in rhythm to the determined movement of his hand molding her breast. She dragged his air into her lungs in gulp after breathless gulp, and tasted his champagne flavor.

He expected her to be experienced, she realized. To understand the proper responses. To know how to please him in return for all of the clamoring feelings he was giving to her.

But she knew none of that. Not really. In this, too, she was a fraud.

A sob rose in her throat. With an effort, she pushed him away and looked into his blazing eyes.

"There's something..." Her breath hitched. "There's something you need to know."

"I hope to God you are not about to change your mind, Princess. There is no possible way I can stop. Not now."

She shook her head. "It's not that. I want to but..."

He covered her face with sweet, hot kisses. "But what, love?"

"I've never..." She swallowed the lump in her throat. "I've never made love before."

André went very still. Her admission struck him like the icy needles of a cold shower. Muscles tensed in regions of his body that had never known such strain. How the hell was he going to go slow enough not to hurt her when he wanted her so much?

André was man enough, with a large enough ego, to realize that by being her first lover he would always hold a special place in her memory. He relished the opportunity to penetrate her maidenhead, and at the same time, cursed his good fortune.

"How is that possible?" he asked, studying her eyes darkened by passion. "Are American men so blind they did not wish to pluck the most glorious flower in the entire land?"

"A few tried," she admitted, nervousness pushing her voice to a higher pitch. "I know it seems silly. Even unbelievable at my age. Particularly to someone like you who's so sophisticated." She heaved out a jagged sigh. "You probably don't think twice about having sex."

He framed her face with his palms. "You're wrong, little one." She had never looked so young and vulnerable, her eyes wide, her breasts straining against her gown with each anxious intake of air. The painful ache in his loins redoubled, but he forced aside his needs. "Whatever you may believe, I take neither women nor sex casually."

"I'm glad," she whispered, her delicate fingers closing around his wrists to keep his hands in place. "My grandmother once said a princess was supposed to go to her marriage bed a virgin. I suppose that's only a part of the fairy tales she spun, but whenever some guy tried to... you know, I thought of her, and I simply couldn't go through with it."

"She must have been a formidable woman to have had such an impact on your life."

"She was. I loved her very much." Tears welled in her eyes. "Do you mind that I'm not exactly an expert at this?"

"Mind?" He dragged his thumb along her lower lip and felt her tremble. From her kisses he knew she was a passionate woman. That she had waited so long to give herself to a man, when she was brimming with her own fires, humbled André. "It will be my greatest pleasure to teach you all that I know."

In a single, agile motion, he lifted her into his arms and carried her up the stairs.

Chapter Nine

A single lamp beside the bed cast a circle of muted light across covers pulled back to reveal pale blue satin sheets. Matching pillows lay side-by-side. Waiting. The thought constricted Nicole's throat and sent her heart off on a wild, primitive beat.

André lowered her slowly down the length of his strong, male body until she stood unsteadily on her feet. Her thoughts seemed to be moving in slow motion, making her acutely aware of the smooth texture of his jacket beneath her fingers, the press of his hard chest against her aching breasts, and a low throbbing sensation between her thighs. His evening whiskers looked dark and rough, thoroughly masculine. His lips curved in invitation as she studied their sensuous shape.

The effort to breath in an ordinary way spasmed her lungs.

"André?"

"Do not be afraid, my beautiful princess." He placed a gentle kiss on top of her head. "Do you remember how you felt before the party? When I brought you the necklace?"

"Yes." The admission scraped up her throat. She'd thought of little else all evening.

"Tell me how it was with you."

To be forced to speak of such intimate, erotic feelings brought a rush of heated blood to her cheeks. "Like I was made of warm liquid. When you looked at me, touched me, I thought I would melt."

"Good." He reached to the back of her neck to unsnap the diamond clasp. "Do you feel that way now?"

"Worse." She smiled. He had the most talented, gentle hands. "Or better. I can't even tell which way is up or down, you have me so confused. You've had me pretty well mixed up since the beginning." She imagined getting kidnapped did that to a woman.

"It has been much the same for me."

"Really?" She hadn't thought it possible she could throw him off balance.

One end of the necklace came free and swung across the top of her breasts like a glittering pendulum. So sensitive was her flesh, every nerve ending flamed. André tossed the jewels onto the dressing table with casual unconcern.

"Shouldn't you put those back in the box?" she asked.

"Later. Right now I have far more important matters on my mind." As he directed his attention to lowering her zipper with his deft fingers, he asked, "During the party, did you imagine what we would be doing now?"

"I'm afraid so." In vivid detail.

"So did I, my love. But because I have more experience, my imagination is no doubt more accurate than yours." Dipping his head, he kissed the side of her neck and nuzzled her ear.

"No doubt," she echoed, her voice shaking.

"Would you like me to tell you what I imagined?"

Her eyes fluttered closed. He could do anything he wanted. Anything at all. "Yes."

"I saw you lying in that big four-poster over there, with your hair loose and spread out across the pillow. Amber ribbons streaming across the satin." As he spoke, his fingers slowly removed the pins that held her hair in place. The strands tumbled down her neck and caressed her bare back. "I imagined you naked, and saw myself kissing you. Everywhere."

He slid one dress sleeve off her shoulder and kissed her there. Warm. Soft. Repeating the process, he worked the other sleeve free. The designer dress, so incredibly elegant, drifted down her body to puddle at her feet.

With his palms, he lifted her breasts, weighing them, his hands sliding along the silk slip that still covered them. "Lovely," he said in a hoarse whisper.

She swallowed hard.

He bent his head to take her right nipple into his mouth, laving it through the sheer fabric until it grew turgid from his ministrations. Nicole gasped and speared her fingers through his hair, pulling him harder against the aching sensation he created. The wonder was she could remain standing since every bone in her body had turned to molten jelly.

When he did the same to the other breast, she sobbed his name. "André, I can't . . ." She couldn't think, or breath, or handle the exquisitely shattering feelings that coursed through her body. Her fingers dug into his scalp. "It's not fair."

"What is not fair, my love?"

"I can't . . . I want to see you, too."

"Ah." Smiling as though outrageously pleased with himself, he shrugged off his jacket, tossing it aside. The cummerbund flew to the floor in a flash of scarlet. When the studs on his shirt wouldn't cooperate, he simply yanked open his shirt, sending tiny diamond buttons scattering all across the room.

She stared at him with unabashed pleasure. As she had expected, dark hair furred his muscular chest and arrowed into hiding below his belt. Tentatively, she ran her fingertips through the crisp curls, noting the deep, rich swirls. When she accidentally touched his nipple, it hardened and André drew in a quick breath. She smiled up at him, relishing a sudden sense of equal partnership. "Is it as exciting for you as it is for me when I touch you like that?"

He caught her wrist. "If you keep it up, you will find out soon enough." Need raked through André with fiery claws. Nicole's innocent willingness to explore his body, as he longed to investigate hers, intensified his painful cravings to know all of her. To hold back would be the ultimate test of his self-control. And yet he knew he must.

The slip she wore was translucent, and where he had suckled at her breasts, the fabric clung to her raised nipples. Tempting him. Inviting his hungry kiss. With an effort, he tempered his urge to lift her in his arms and swiftly bury himself in her hot core. The image lured him, but he struggled to recall her sweet virginity, not *his* needs.

Taking her by the arm, he led her to the bed. She was offering him a precious gift she had given to no other. He recognized the danger in his acceptance, the responsibility that came with the giving and taking of virginity. A part of him knew Nicole might be better off if he left her alone. But that was a sacrifice he was unable to make. Not tonight. Not while his blood raged so hot, his need like a steel shaft of pain.

He tried not to think about the changes he would wrought in both Nicole and himself by even the most careful of takings. The risks were great; the benefits outweighed them all, he realized as he contemplated the dark arousal in her eyes, her innocent willingness. The knowledge that she wanted him with as much passion as he desired her was as exhilarating as flooring the accelerator around a tight curve. The natural forces were irresistible, and nearly spun him out of control.

With shaky hands, he removed the rest of her clothing, fisting the lacy undergarments as he fought for control. He had never known a more beautiful or naturally sensuous woman. Even her light tan line stretching between her slender hips enhanced rather than detracted from her perfection.

Nicole lay back to observe André as he shed the rest of his clothes. In contrast to her overheated flesh, the satin sheets felt cool and erotically slippery. She had seen male nudity before. At least, statues and little boys playing in front yard sprinklers during the summer. Even a poster male or two on calendars. But she'd never seen a man fully aroused except in clinical texts. The sight of André as he pulled off his briefs took her breath away. How would he ever fit inside her?

She had little time to consider the question as he lay down beside her, his hands starting to stroke her in wonderful, sensual ways.

"Should we turn off the light?" she asked between soft little moans that somehow escaped her throat on their own.

"No, love. To see is to enjoy all the more."

How could she focus on anything with her vision swirling with each new caress and her body throbbing? It was as if rivers of fine metals raced through her...molten silver brilliant and flashing, the warmth of bronze flowing through her veins, and fiery gold so bright it blinded her... blinded her to everything except André. His hands. His lips. His fingers when they slipped between her thighs.

Her muscles clenched and her eyes flew open. "André?"

"Shh, little one. I am simply checking to see if you are ready."

Never before had she understood the true meaning of intimacy. To have a man touch her...there. At the very thought, her heart lurched against her ribs.

And then he did it again, deeper, with a cool slickness that moved back and forth in a blatant invasion of her person. A welcome incursion, she admitted. But so terribly new and unfamiliar. Perversely, at some very basic level, she recognized her total vulnerability to the man for whom she was allowing this ultimate intimacy, and at the same time rejoiced it was the man she loved.

She flinched again when he mounted her, spreading her thighs wide. Taking a deep breath, she fought a rising sense of panic. "I'm sorry. I should be more experienced for you."

"No, Princess. Just as you are is perfect."

He began his penetration then, slowly, allowing her time to accommodate his size. She forced herself to relax and found herself taking him deeper, inch by inch, until the stretching became a sudden burning sensation. She cried out.

"Shh, love. That is all the pain there is. Now there is only pleasure."

He kissed her deeply, making her forget everything else until she realized he was right. A promising warmth replaced the discomfort. Slowly the heat built. She picked up the rhythm of his rocking motions, panting in cadence, scoring his back with her fingernails. She felt herself striving toward some new goal, a destination she'd only read about, and then it was upon her in a burst of joy. On a sob, she called his name. Her body convulsed. Dear God, what power had André unleashed?

An instant later, he pulsed within her and she knew she would never be the same.

A COLD PREMONITION slid along Nicole's spine with the arrival of dawn. This was too good to last.

She snuggled against André's muscular body, feeling the regular rhythm of his breathing move through his chest. She didn't want the warm, honeyed languor to leave her, or to lose the musky scent of sex that filled her nostrils and the sweet flavor of André still lingering on her tongue. He had taught her more about passion than she had ever expected to learn, but in her twenty-eight years she had absorbed other lessons. Bitter pills about dreams that didn't come true.

She wanted to cling to her hope that she had found her prince, that she was indeed his princess. But he always seemed so totally in control, as though she couldn't quite touch his core. Meanwhile, he used his seductive skills so expertly, she simply came apart in his hands.

Closing her eyes, she let herself dream of growing old with André. She pictured those three children the Gypsy woman had foretold, each one dark-haired and smiling back at her with André's cocky grin. Not that she expected to wake up this morning to find herself pregnant. André had taken precautions to prevent that. Though she was in many ways grateful for his foresight, she wondered if his motive was to avoid an unnecessary complication when it was time for her to go home.

Home. A tiny apartment on the west side of L.A. Hardly equal to a near palace set dramatically on a hill overlooking acres of green farmland. To protect her precarious heart, she had to remember where she belonged.

She dragged a shaky breath through her lungs. Dear God how she would miss all of this.

No, she amended with a sharp stab of awareness. The only thing she would truly miss would be André.

"Good morning, Princess."

His voice was morning rough and scratchy, a sound Nicole wished she'd be able to hear with every dawn for the rest of her life. "Did I wake you?"

He toyed with the ends of her hair where it draped across his bare chest. "I cannot imagine a more pleasant way to wake up than to have you in my arms."

"Hmm. Thank you for last night."

"My pleasure, *madame.*" He brushed a kiss to her forehead. "Do you think your grandmother would have approved?"

"Well, we *are* married." However temporarily. "She'd approve of that. And certainly I feel more like a princess now than I ever have before." Being in André's embrace had far more of an effect on her than the elegant room, or people bowing over her hand.

"Tell me about her."

"My grandmother?" Nicole forced herself to think of something other than the way he had lifted one leg over hers and settled his knee between her thighs. "Let's see . . . She wasn't very tall. She loved to tell stories about the Old Country. Margolis, I guess, because that's where she said she was born. And I remember she always jingled when she talked because she wore a lot of bracelets on her arms and loved to gesture wildly." Nicole smoothed the crisp curls on André's chest as she spoke. "In a way, Petra reminded me of her. Everywhere she went, you could hear her music."

"Then your grandmother is the reason you came to my country seeking antiques?"

"I suppose." Though not necessarily on a conscious level. "All those stories she told when I was a child stayed with me. After she died, I never stopped missing her. Maybe I came to Margolis hoping to find her essence again."

His chest vibrated with a low, rumbling laugh. "Instead, *I* found you."

"Yes." Closing her eyes, she pictured that moment on the cathedral steps, and felt again the forbidden thrill of excitement.

"And your mother?" he persisted with another question.

Nicole's fingers stilled. "She had too many dreams that never came true."

"We all have some of those."

Wondering if he was thinking about the woman he had lost to his brother, Nicole shifted her position to see his face more clearly. She was struck once again by his strong profile, classically formed with a straight nose and determined jaw. He could easily have modeled for a bust of a Roman centurion, and driven women crazy in any century.

"What are your dreams, André?"

"At the moment?" With a brash, arrogant grin, he lifted himself onto one elbow and looked down at her. His wayward lock of hair drifted across his forehead. "To make love to you until noon."

"Why the time limit?" she asked impishly, her body already responding to his suggestion.

"Because that is when I am due at a meeting of the Hog Farmers' Cooperative."

She giggled. "You're kidding."

"According to Sebastian, hog farmers represent 2.6 percent of the voters. I would not dare overlook them."

Linking her arms around his neck, she drew his head toward hers. "I'd be delighted to meet all of your constituents."

"Not today, sweetheart. It is too dangerous."

"I wasn't exactly volunteering to get to know the pigs up close and personal."

"It is Hendrik's thugs I worry about, not barnyard animals."

"We'll take the bodyguards along. He won't try anything."

He skimmed his hand over her breast, sending a curl of warmth to her midsection. "You stay home and rest, Princess. I expect you will need all of your energy again this evening. For me."

"But I want to help you win the election. I can't do you any good if you keep me locked up in a cage."

"If I had my way, I would keep you wrapped in silks and satins." He swirled his tongue around her already puckered nipple. "And then I would remove each garment, slowly." He laved again. "Knowing that you are safe is very important to me."

Other things were important to Nicole, but at the moment she had trouble remembering them. Her most basic instincts took command of her thoughts. André. His hands. His lips. The long, hard length of him, and the tender heat he created between her thighs.

BY THE NEXT DAY, André discovered the members of the classic car club were as unable to hold his attention as the hog farmers had been the previous day. And he still had to make a scheduled visit to the ladies' auxiliary of the fire department to ask for their support in the election before he could go home to his wife.

Wife. Nicole had so totally insinuated herself in his life she was all he thought about—day and night. He used to linger over a beer with Sebastian at the end of a day. Or compare notes on fuel-injected carburetors with the mechanics in town. He had even been known to indulge in a temporary liaison with a willing woman for the sheer pleasure of female companionship.

All of those distractions paled in comparison to being with Nicole for a single hour. She *was* changing him, and in a way that frightened him.

Even so, during the remainder of the campaign his schedule was so tight he would have little time to devote to the pursuit he most enjoyed. Nicole.

BY THE THIRD DAY of being kept in a silk-lined, gilded cage, Nicole knew exactly what was wrong. Though her nights with André were filled with sensuous delights, during the day she was as useless as a decorative ornament. Inactivity grated on her. She simply couldn't play the grand dame waiting game a moment longer. If André didn't want her as a helpmate in his political career, she'd be damned if she'd sit on her butt all day. She had her own life to lead.

Her personal bodyguard, thoroughly bored with his job, had taken to spending most of his time in the kitchen. Probably trying to hit on Katja just to pass the time.

Dressed in a summer skirt and knit top, Nicole slipped out of the house into the garage. She'd found the keys to the Rolls-Royce tossed carelessly in a jewelry tray in André's room. She wanted to visit a flea market in a little town not far away. With luck, she'd be there and back before André, or even her bodyguard, knew she was gone.

The car started easily.

As she backed out, she smiled to herself. Who would have thought little Nikki LeDeaux would be out shopping for antiques in a Rolls-Royce town car?

The flea market didn't have much to offer, though she did pick up a stunning pair of blue enameled candlesticks for the equivalent of pennies. This scouring Europe for good buys wasn't as hard as she had feared. In fact, she was damn good at it.

As she was passing a street vendor with a pile of miscellaneous merchandise, an old wooden box caught her eye. It was roughly made, but opening lids was a habit she'd long since honed. You simply never knew what might be inside.

To her delight, the box was filled with old mechanic's tools. They didn't have much intrinsic value, but she immediately pictured them attractively displayed on the wall of André's garage, like a dentist might show off historical tools of his trade. A little scrubbing, some varnish to make them shine. She'd mount them in a shadow box lined with hand-stamped metal, and they'd be perfect.

When she took her purchases back to the car, she discovered she wasn't ready to give up her freedom just yet and return to her gilded cage, otherwise known as the House of Montiard. It was far too nice a day. The worst of the summer heat had moderated, and a light breeze teased at the fine hairs along the nape of her neck. She'd find her way to Petra's antique store, she decided. There were probably layers of goodies underneath the piles of trash she hadn't yet examined.

"WHERE IS that handsome husband of yours?" Petra asked as she swept into the cluttered room in response to the tinkling of the bell on the front door.

"Out doing his political thing." Nicole smiled. The old Gypsy did act a lot like her grandmother—excitable and flamboyant.

"Tell him he must see me at once. His signs are becoming quite confused. I fear the omens are bad."

"I'm not sure André believes in fortune-telling."

"Of course not. Why should he? He is a *gaje*."

Nicole blanched. Her grandmother had always accused Nicole's mother of wanting to rise above herself. But that had been so long ago, Nicole had forgotten the word—and the derisive way it was said, as though the town were about to be overrun by a horde of cockroaches.

"I thought I'd look around a little more," she said, though she had a sudden impulse to run out the door as fast as she could.

"As you wish, though I am surprised your husband allows you out on your own."

Nicole pushed aside a stack of poorly embroidered waist sashes to examine a china plate, which turned out to be chipped. "Why not? I'm a grown woman." And she doubted Petra was aware of the threat from Hendrik.

"Montiard women do not mix with the rest of us." She raised her nose in an exaggerated way. "Either their men do not let them out, or they are too snooty."

In spite of herself, a laugh escaped Nicole's throat. "I don't think I qualify as snooty."

"No, Princess. You are definitely one of us."

Us? As in Gypsy? She gave a mental shake of her head. That wasn't possible. Nicole's mother would have vehemently denied even the suggestion she was of Gypsy birth. In fact, Nicole could vaguely remember her mother and grandmother arguing—No, she wasn't going to think about that. The whole idea gave her a decidedly uncomfortable feeling in the pit of her stomach.

She shouldn't have come back to Petra's store.

After making only a perfunctory tour of the shop, Nicole left, but Petra's words continued to haunt her. The Gypsy woman had triggered some deep memory that conjured up conflicting emotions. For the moment, Nicole felt she had enough on her plate without having to deal with her past.

THE INSTANT she saw André's Ferrari parked in the garage, and realized he'd beaten her home, she sensed things were not going to go well. The fact that he was standing with his arms crossed, a deepening scowl on his face simply confirmed her suspicions.

"Where the hell have you been?" he questioned as she got out of the car and retrieved her packages from the back seat.

"Shopping," she said reasonably.

"Alone?"

"That's right. I've been known to go on my own to any number of places—the grocery store, shopping malls, even halfway around the world."

"Where did you go this time?"

"Is this an inquisition?"

"No, damn it!"

The clasp on the toolbox popped open, the tools clattered to the garage floor, and she was left standing there with an empty box banging against her leg. "It sure as hell sounds like it."

He grabbed her and his fingers dug into her shoulders. She'd never seen him angry before, or at least not since she'd tried to escape in the old farmer's wagon and been caught by Hendrik's goons. But this was different. André's fury was decidedly directed at her. His eyes blazed with barely controlled rage. A muscle rippled in his jaw. "You are not supposed to leave the estate without a bodyguard."

"I'm tired of being a prisoner. Hendrik isn't going to try anything now. We're married. The whole world knows that. It would be political suicide." She tried to shrug away from him but he wouldn't let her go. "I'm not used to being a princess on some damn pedestal. Let me help in your campaign, or the devil is going to find work for idle hands. Count on it."

"Like flaunting yourself in front of every villager from here to the border?"

"I don't flaunt. I wouldn't even know how." Where in the world had that accusation come from?

They glared at each other for a dozen heartbeats. With a tilt of her chin, she dared him to argue with her. She was a real person, not someone to be controlled by his whims, or even by some cretin like Hendrik.

"Then what the hell are all those greasy tools for?"

"They're a present. For you, you jerk! I was going to mount them and hang them over your workbench. I was *trying* to be a thoughtful wife. Next time, I won't bother."

"Princess." The hoarse whisper of her name tore at her equilibrium.

He shoved her into the plush velvet back seat of the car. The rest of her packages clattered to the floorboard.

With blatant intimacy, he raised her skirt to her waist. His hand slid between her thighs, kneading, roughing her with his palm. She shoved at his shoulders and his dark eyes locked with hers. "You are my wife." He ground the words out from between clenched teeth.

"Yes. And damn it, I love you!"

The words struck André with the power of a summer storm. What had begun in anger and blind jealousy—and fear for her safety, he admitted—became a slow, sensuous assault. He slid her panties down her thighs, freeing her nest of auburn curls to his sight, to his kiss, and to the sweet torture of his tongue.

She moaned, raking her fingers through his hair, until he rose above her, sheathing himself in her moist heat. As though she could not get enough of him, she ripped his shirt open, and scored her nails across his chest.

"Nicole." The word tore from his throat.

"You don't own me." The passion in her eyes was so dark there was nothing there except black irises circled in green gold.

"No. Never." He kissed her, deep, hungry probes that had her arching to him, devouring him, until he felt her shudder and tighten around him. He had never known a woman like this, never realized how much he wanted to hear her words of love. As her contractions squeezed him to sweet, tortuous release, he cried her name out loud, then sank into her welcoming flesh, oblivious to where they were or how roughly he had taken her.

That night in bed, he stroked her supple body in the aftermath of a much quieter lovemaking.

"There is a ribbon cutting tomorrow," he said. "At a home for the elderly. Would you care to join me?"

She sighed. "Absolutely." He was back in control, she mused, but that afternoon he'd totally lost it. He hadn't bothered with sweet seduction. He'd been belligerent, domineering, possessive, and jealous. By damn, in spite of herself, she'd loved it. Because he'd shown he cared.

THE NEEDLE craft guild. War veterans' home. Friends of the Library. Carpenters' union hall. Opening day at a racetrack.

In the past two weeks, Nicole had been to them all, plus assorted handshaking opportunities at grocery stores and barnyards. André was forced to campaign in more than just his own parliamentary district. He had to gain support for his party's candidates all over the country if he hoped to get enough votes to unseat Hendrik. Which meant, in André's case, he needed to carry on fifty-one separate campaigns to assure twenty-six wins to claim victory.

Never in her entire life had Nicole met so many strangers. Her face actually ached with the effort to keep smiling. Her feet were swollen two sizes larger than her shoes.

Desperate to get away from the press of the crowd—a hundred hot, sweaty bodies belonging to members of the Society for the Preservation of Native Margolis Dances—she slipped out the side door of the village social hall. The cool evening air made her shiver and she rubbed her arms.

How did André do it? she wondered, a weary sigh escaping as she looked into the night sky. Day after day, his smile never slipped. He pressed so much flesh, it was amazing he could still shake hands at all. He had more energy than ten men determined to beat Hendrik at his own political game.

Then, just when Nicole was ready to fall into exhausted sleep after a grueling day, André still had enough energy to make love to her half the night. Not that she objected, she thought with a satisfied smile.

Nor did she truly mind all the attention she received as heir to the throne, she admitted. Little by little she could feel herself getting used to the role, and liking it.

And she liked helping André, too. Each day she could feel support for him building among the people. *Her* people, she mused.

A chorus of crickets chirped in the shrubbery that surrounded the social hall and in the distance she heard a dog bark. She thought about L.A. where there was always a ambient hum of traffic, and the few stars you could see were dimmed by reflected city lights. To her surprise, rural life suited her.

A car rounded the corner of the building and the flash of headlights blinded her. As the vehicle pulled to a stop, she heard car doors open.

Squinting, she tried to see who was there.

Two large, hulking shapes walked toward her through the beam of light. She backed toward the side entrance to the social hall.

"Good evening, *madame*. If you would be so kind, there is someone who would like to speak with you."

Nicole started to scream but a big meaty hand covered her mouth. She struggled to escape. It was no good. The guy was a giant. Just before he stuffed her into the back seat of a black Citroën, Nicole kicked one of her shoes loose.

She hoped to goodness her prince would come looking for her soon.

Chapter Ten

André made his way to Sebastian's side through a crush of dancers dressed in colorful peasant costumes. They swayed to violins playing syrupy romantic music, accompanied by the soft click of castanets.

"Where is Nicole?" he asked his campaign manager. Like André, sweat dampened his friend's white shirt and his coat and tie had long since been discarded in the overheated room.

Sebastian lifted his shoulders in an unconcerned shrug. "She was here a minute ago talking with the soloist dancer. Perhaps she went to powder her nose?"

"What about the bodyguards? It is their job to watch her." He checked over his shoulder to see one of the guards standing at his post by the entrance. No alarm had been sounded, no shout had announced a problem. Still, he did not like having Nicole out of his sight.

"You worry too much, my friend. What could happen with all of these people around?"

André wasn't sure. But he did know the short hairs at the back of his neck were trying to tell him something. He intended to find his wife. Now. If he had listened to his instincts a year ago, maybe Christian and his family would still be alive.

He shoved through the door to the hallway. The solo dancer strutted toward him.

"Ah, Monsieur Montiard." She smiled and fluttered her dark eye lashes. "I trust you enjoyed my performance."

"Wonderful. Do you know where my wife is?"

"No, but I do know where there is a private room where we could—"

He brushed past her into the ladies' room. Another dancer stood preening before the mirror, her eyes widening in surprise as he checked the empty stalls.

Damn! Where could Nicole have gone?

He checked with the bodyguards, who claimed ignorance when he found Sebastian again, he fisted his shirt collar around his scrawny neck. "She is gone, you son of an anthill! You and your army were supposed to be looking after Nicole."

"Easy, André." Coughing, Sebastian wrested free of the choke hold. "She is probably outside getting some air. Who wouldn't leave this oven if they could?" He pointedly wiped away a sheen of perspiration from his forehead.

"She would not have left without telling me."
Time and again, André had warned her of the dangers that could potentially nip at their heels. How could she have forgotten?

"Come on, you old married man," Sebastian said, smirking. "If I had known wedded bliss would make you so foul tempered, I would not have suggested such a drastic measure in order to beat Meier-Wahl."

André grabbed up his jacket, but before he could make his way outside to search for Nicole, Robert von Helman caught him by the arm.

"I need to talk with you," the reporter insisted, his expression grim.

Fear clutched at André. "Is it something about Nicole?"

"Her background. My sources in the States—"

"Unless you know where she is right now, I will have to talk to you later. I must find her."

"She is missing?"

He scanned the room once more. "Maybe she is out back." Or if his instincts were working, maybe something else had happened less pleasant than going outside for a cool breath of air.

He shoved out the door. Some of the partygoers were starting to leave. They milled around the exit, saying last-minute goodbyes, then heading for their cars. Headlights flashed across the parking lot. None of them picked out the regal young woman André sought.

"Sebastian, have the guards check around back," he ordered. "Robert, you cover the parking lot. Do not leave a stone unturned." His friends hurried to do as instructed while André took the quiet side of the social hall where a gravel driveway led to an old maintenance shed. The shadows were deep next to the wooden structure, the bushes thick. He was about to fetch a flashlight from his car when he saw the shoe.

He held the soft leather in his hands as he fought the terror that thrummed through his body. His fear had weight and it pressed down on his shoulders, shifting his vision and knotting his stomach. His fingers twitched with the desire to strangle.

Hendrik.

HIS RACE along dark country roads in his speeding Ferrari was an instinctive act born of desperation. Without apparent effort, his keen sense of direction and timing kept him on course to Hendrik's mountain retreat. He focused entirely on Nicole—willing her to be safe, ignoring the fact he pursued her alone. At some very basic level, he knew bringing an army of guards along would put Nicole at even greater risk.

A plan formed as he approached Hendrik's hunting lodge. André knew the area well. He had played here as a boy. Now he would draw on all that knowledge to slip past the guards to save his wife.

Wife. The word washed over him as easily as a car accelerates on a banked turn. There was a natural grace to the single syllable, a smooth, solid feeling filled with both hope and anticipation.

Parking the Ferrari well away from the lodge, he moved stealthily through the forest. Pine needles muffled his footsteps. A single light glowing from a downstairs window gave him direction as he dodged from the shadow of one tree to the next. On invisible air currents, the careless scent of tobacco smoke gave away the guard's location, allowing André to skirt through the darkness to the other side of the half-timbered building.

An open window was all he needed.

Levering himself inside, he dropped to all fours.

In the adjacent room he heard voices, a man and woman speaking in low, intimate tones. Glasses clinked, followed by the sound of feminine laughter.

Fury raged through André. What the hell was Nicole up to? Or had Hendrik already drugged her?

He rested his hand on the doorknob, took a deep breath, then burst into the neighboring room.

"Do not try anything, Hendrik, or so help me—" André stopped in his tracks and stared at the nearly naked woman sitting on the couch next to the prime minister. "Who the hell is she?"

"Henny, honey, who is this dreadful man?" The brunette scrambled to find something to cover her rather ample endowments.

With considerable aplomb, Hendrik stood and buckled his pants. His gray hair was thoroughly mussed, and he failed to so much as blush. "What is this all about, Montiard? For a social call, your timing is dismal."

"It is not social, you blackguard. What have you done with Nicole?"

The woman started to get up from the couch. "If you have business, Henny, I'll just—"

"Shut up, Bipsy."

Henny? Bipsy? "What the hell is going on?" André felt as though he had come into the middle of a movie and missed an important part of the plot. "Where is Nicole?"

"I assure you, young man, even I can handle only one woman at a time. If your wife is missing, you will have to look for her elsewhere."

André shot a glance from the woman to Hendrik and back again. "Nicole's not here?"

"That is precisely what I have been trying to tell you." Hendrik finished tucking his shirttail into his trousers. "I assume you can find your own way out."

André got right in Hendrik's face, so close he could smell the faint scent of wine on his breath. He gritted his teeth and his fingers flexed into fists. "My wife is missing. I am not leaving here until you tell me where she is."

"I have never had any interest in keeping track of your wife's whereabouts. If she were smart, instead of a fraudulent imposter, she would have gone back to the States weeks ago."

"Someone has kidnapped her."

The brunette gasped. "Oh, dear."

"I am not responsible for her coming up missing any more than I was guilty of throwing a pipe bomb in some farmer's house, or in causing your brother's accident. I grow more than weary of your accusations."

"Your men, then."

Hendrik shook his head. "I never gave any such orders."

But someone had, André realized. With Hendrik fully occupied with the brunette, it stood to reason he was not involved in Nicole's disappearance. And maybe there was a remote possibility he was not behind the other incidents either.

André speared his fingers through his hair. If not Hendrik, then who?

Half an hour later, he found himself shinnying up the outside drainpipe of an apartment house. The plaster ripped at his pant legs. Without gloves, jagged edges of the rotted sheet metal tore at his hands. If he was wrong—or if the damn pipe broke off—he would feel like a fool, or worse.

But if he was right, Nicole was in serious danger.

NICOLE WATCHED her captor with a wary eye. "Is there something genetic about Margolians that makes them want to kidnap people?"

"You do not understand." Pacing across the living room of the third-floor apartment on the outskirts of downtown San Margo, Marlene Marquette presented the picture of agitation. Her platinum-blond hair had come loose from its staid French braid and strands dragged haphazardly at her neck. Her red-rimmed eyes glistened. "I am giving you a chance to get away from André before it is too late."

"Why would I want to do that?" Nicole questioned cautiously. The room was filled with cheap replicas and tasteless decorations in futile imitation of elegance. She still wasn't sure why Hendrik's thugs had brought her to this tawdry apartment, instead of directly to the prime minister.

"It is obvious. The man forced you to marry him, did he not?"

"That's true." Though Nicole's relationship with André had changed rather substantially in the interim, at least from her perspective. The fact that André had said nothing about a permanent commitment didn't mean it was outside the realm of possibility. Or perhaps Nicole was developing into an eternal optimist in her old age.

"André is dangerous. Surely as a woman you have sensed that."

"In a way." Mostly André was perilous to Nicole's heart, but she wasn't going to admit to that. "He's not exactly a violent person." Sexy, seductive, and devilishly handsome were far better descriptions.

"No? Then you are not aware he killed his brother and his family?"

Nicole went very still. She recalled Hendrik had made a similar remark. "I don't believe you."

"The brakes failed on Christian's car. That is how they died, in a terrible, fiery crash. Who do you think did all of the maintenance work on the car?" she asked, flipping the loose strands of her hair behind her shoulder. "Who knew every nut, bolt and washer?"

"André?"

"That is why you must leave now. Before it is too late." The woman shoved an airplane ticket into Nicole's hands.

"Did Hendrik put you up to this?"

"No, no. It is because I care about you. Trust me, I have your best interests at heart."

Sure. Just like a con man cares about his mark.
"Why would André want to kill his brother?"

"You Americans are so naive. He was driven by jealousy and greed. Why does any man do what he does?"

"You're wrong about André." She'd bet her life on it.

Wringing her hands, Marlene sat heavily on an ottoman across from Nicole. "Poor André was the second son. That meant he had inherited almost nothing from his father. By killing Christian and his entire family, he could have it all."

"You mean, he was broke?"

"Well, perhaps not as you mean it. He did, of course, have some small money of his own. A few million francs." She tossed the number aside with a casual sweep of her hand. "But the land, and all that goes with it, belonged to his brother."

"I don't think André cares all that much about money. And I don't think he's the jealous type." Of course, she couldn't know that for sure. There had indeed been a few moments when she'd felt his possessive hand at her back. Not unpleasantly, for the most part.

"Oh, you are wrong. He loved my sister, Monique, and was furious with her. When she threw him over for Christian..." Marlene's eyes glistened even more brightly. "I told him all along Monique was not right for him. And finally...*she had to die.*" She spat out the venomous pronouncement.

Nicole flinched at the woman's fury. She desperately wished André would show up and get her out of this mess. Men were never around when you needed them. Of course, there was no possible way he would know she was here. When he discovered she'd been snatched, he'd probably head right for Hendrik. Meanwhile, she was stuck chatting with a woman who was definitely unpredictable and probably dangerous.

"Maybe you misunderstood André's motives," Nicole suggested. *And are too wrapped up in some terrible jealousy of your own to think rationally,* she left unsaid.

Marlene made a low, feral sound deep in her throat. "You cannot have him. André is mine. He always has been." Her eyes flared with an insane gleam. Leaping to her feet, she whipped a curving, serrated knife from the folds of her skirt. "If you will not leave, then I will have to kill you, too."

Nicole's throat constricted. "You won't get away with this," she warned. She squirmed her way up and over the back of the couch, putting the ugly piece of furniture between herself and the madwoman. Glancing around, she looked for some sort of a weapon, anything to protect herself.

Marlene tracked her around the end of the couch.

Panic mixed with rising terror. Picking up a pillow, Nicole used it as a shield. "I've reconsidered. Going back to the States sounds like a wonderful idea. Can't imagine why I didn't think of it myself." Her breath lodged in her lungs, making the words sound erratic and high-pitched.

"Do not lie to me, you little bitch." The knife sliced through the pillow like she was gutting a pig. "Monique lied to me. That is why she died, you know. I saw to that."

Tossing the shredded pillow at her assailant, Nicole screamed and made a dash for the door. She fumbled with the double locks. One turned easily, but the other one stuck. The sound of Marlene's deranged laughter filled the room and ricocheted inside Nicole's head. Her heart beat adrenaline through her veins with rocket force. Her hands shook.

Sensing the woman's hot breath on her neck, Nicole ducked, but not fast enough. The knife sliced through the fabric of her dress, ripping a jagged tear. Knees weak, Nicole stumbled away from the crazed woman. The next time she might not be so lucky.

Dear God, I don't want to die.

Glass shattered on the opposite side of the room and Marlene's laughter turned to a wail.

Nicole whirled.

She almost collapsed in relief to see André stagger up from where he'd fallen onto the floor and wrestle the knife from Marlene's hand. Window glass lay in shards across the carpeting.

The woman clawed and kicked at him, crying and sobbing. "I love you, André. I did all of this for you. For us! Do you not see how much I love you."

Wrapping his arms tightly around Marlene in a bear hug, his breathing coming hard, he restrained her until her cries grew weaker and muffled against his chest. His bones ached from his exertion, yet he hated the pitiful noises she made, the anguish her every movement communicated. He had never meant to hurt her, had never expected her love to become so terribly distorted. Certainly he had hoped she would outgrow her adolescent infatuation. Guilt for her misunderstanding twisted through his gut.

"Monique was not right for you, my love," Marlene sobbed. "She was not right for you. I am the only one..."

"Shh," he whispered.

Over the top of the weeping woman's head, Nicole noted André's expression filled with compassion. "Call an ambulance," he ordered calmly as he met her gaze.

Unsteadily, she went to the phone on the end table and dialed zero. After she'd gotten her message through, she sank into a nearby chair, put her head in her hands, and let her own tears flow freely down her cheeks.

NICOLE'S HEAD still throbbed two hours later as she and André watched the police car drive away in the same direction as the ambulance that had earlier taken Marlene to the hospital, probably to the psychiatric ward. Sedated, Marlene had looked almost angelic as the gurney slipped into the back door of the emergency vehicle—except for the flashing red light slashing rhythmically across her beautiful features.

Shivering in the night air, and pulling André's suit jacket more tightly around her shoulders, Nicole said, "I still don't understand how you knew where to find me."

"When I confronted Hendrik and realized he was not the real villain in the piece, I mentally started at the beginning. Sebastian heard about you from almost the moment you arrived in the country. Marlene, since she was so close to Hendrik, had always been one of his inside sources for information." He slid his arm across Nicole's shoulder, ushering her toward his car. "When I remembered Marlene's father is a customs officer, everything else began to make sense."

"That surly customs man was her father? I remember your grandmother saying Christian's wife had a father who was a minor government official."

"Right. He apparently called Marlene directly, not Hendrik, as I had suspected. She was acting on her own when she sent those thugs after you. Trying to protect her employer, I imagine. Only things backfired for her."

"You married me. I'm sure that wasn't in her plan." With a sigh, she shook her head. "Poor jealous woman. How she must have hated it when she learned what had happened."

"Enough to try to frighten you off with that pipe bomb, it seems. When that did not work, she came up with tonight's stunt."

"Which reminds me, where did you find the ladder to get to the second-floor window?"

His lips lifted into a cocky grin. "For us hero types, triflings like ladders are unnecessary. Naturally, I would scale the highest wall bare-handed to rescue a damsel in distress."

She laughed. Getting an honest answer out of him seemed unlikely. She was simply grateful he had arrived in time.

André opened the car door for Nicole and she gratefully slid into the passenger seat, sinking with bone-weary tiredness into the rich leather. The elegant upholstery had the same seductive scent as the car's owner, she mused.

Before he could start the car, she touched him on the arm. "She accused you of killing your brother."

Nicole felt him stiffen. "Did you believe her?"

"No."

He turned to her. "Just like that? No? At the time, half the country questioned my guilt. A good many still do."

"You loved your brother and you didn't have any reason to kill him."

"How about money?"

"André, you've never worked a day in your life—at least not for pay—and you spend money like it grows on trees. I can't imagine a few million francs one way or the other would mean a diddly damn to you."

He laughed, a low, warm chuckle. "You are right, of course. Now, a motor that is humming at twenty-five hundred RPM without a hiccup... that is worth something." His smile dissolved. "But there is another matter..."

"Monique?"

"You know about her?"

"I know you once loved her, before she married Christian." Nicole glanced away, afraid to watch his expression too closely. "Did you still love her when she died?"

"No. I found my sister-in-law had a rather serious fault, not uncommon to a great many women."

She shot him a curious look.

"She was unfaithful to Christian. Oh, not with me," he added quickly. "I am only grateful my brother never learned of her deception."

Small wonder André had so little faith in women. Deserted as a child by his mother, and then doubly deceived by the woman he loved.

"André, about Marlene..."

He twisted the key in the ignition. "There was never anything between us. At least, not on my part. She liked to hang around in the garage while I worked, so I taught her what I knew as a way to find something to talk about. Clearly I underestimated her feelings, an oversight I now regret." He pulled away from the curb and headed down the deserted street. A yellow cat on a midnight prowl scampered out of the way.

"Would Marlene have known enough about cars to sabotage your brother's and cause the accident?"

He drove in silence a few minutes, taking them out of town onto the highway. "Marlene would have known." The words seemed to drag in a painful tremor from his throat. "Dear God, I never considered that possibility. That means...in a way...the accident *was* my fault."

Nicole rested a consoling hand on his thigh. There was little she could say that would ease his grief. The night had been mentally and physically exhausting for them both. Leaning her head back, she closed her eyes. The last thing she felt before she drifted off to

sleep was André's hand covering hers, warm and reassuring, and thoroughly masculine.

When she woke, it was to a bright dawn casting the
early rays of sunlight through an enchanted forest.
Tucked among stately pines and aspen crowned with
golden leaves, a gabled cottage glistened white like a
nostalgic scene out of Hansel and Gretel.

As the sun caressed the tops of the pines, a dove
cooed softly and was answered by its companion.
Along the front of the porch, trailing morning glories opened their white and blue petals to greet the
day.

Chapter Eleven

"Where are we?" Blinking and stretching like a cat just coming awake, Nicole raised her head from André's shoulder.

With the back of his fingers, he brushed her sleep-mussed hair away from her face. Her cheek felt warm and incredibly soft. Muscles tightened in his groin at the renewed realization of how close he had come to losing her. "It is my secret hideaway, my own little private bit of the Margolian alps."

"The house looks as if it's right out of a fairy tale," she said on a sigh.

He placed a soft kiss on her forehead. "So do you. Sleeping Beauty comes to mind."

"Are you sure I don't look more like the wicked witch?" she asked, her laugh low and sultry. "My hair must be a fright. And my clothes are wrinkled and ripped." She glanced at a jagged tear in her blouse.

Something sharp twisted through his gut, as if a knife had cut through his own flesh. "Thank God, you were not hurt. I am not sure I could have—"

"I'm fine. Really. But I feel a mess."

"You are lovely." More beautiful than any woman he had ever known, and more desirable.

"When we left Marlene's apartment . . ." Her hazel eyes clouded at the memory. "I assumed we were going home. To the House of Montiard. Why did we come here?"

"No one knows I own Dove's Roost except Sebastian, and he is sworn to secrecy on penalty of loosing his free beer ticket. You need a chance to recover from your ordeal. After what happened last night, the press will be in a feeding frenzy and you would never get any rest. We will let Hendrik field questions about the excesses of his staff member while we remain unavailable for comment."

"But what about your campaign? You have dozens of scheduled appearances."

"Sebastian will cancel them." While Nicole had slept in the car, André had stopped at a phone booth to call his friend with instructions as to how to handle matters in his absence. "Since the polls are shifting in my favor, a few days will not matter. And Hendrik will be kept busy handling damage control to protect his own campaign."

Frowning, she palmed his cheek in a caring caress. He was struck again by how easily she had believed he was not responsible for Christian's death.

Not many women would have had so much faith in a man they had met only weeks ago.

"You look exhausted," she said. "You must have driven all night."

"We will have plenty of time to rest. And..." The word hung on a suggestive note.

She raised her eyebrows in question.

"And fish, of course."

She choked back a laugh.

He grinned at the way she'd fallen for his innuendo. "Native trout," he explained. "Wily creatures. Very difficult to catch." He got out of the car and walked around to her side.

"In Beverly Hills, fish come from the supermarket."

Opening the door, he picked her up in his arms and carried her toward the house. "Then you have a real treat in store, Princess. There is nothing more enjoyable than feeling a fish tug on your line and then setting the hook. Except perhaps..." He let his voice trail off as he worked the door open.

"Except perhaps what?" She nuzzled her face against his neck and he caught the lingering scent of her floral perfume.

"Making love to you."

"Hmm. I like the sound of that."

He carried her across the threshold and lowered her to her feet. "Welcome to Dove's Roost." The words came out in a hoarse whisper. Until now, no woman had entered his secret hideaway, no woman had meant so much to him as Nicole. André had an urge to lock the door behind them and never let her go.

Framing her face between his hands, he studied each feature in exquisite detail—the flecks of gold in her hazel eyes, the pert tilt of her nose, the inviting shape of her lips. But simply looking at her for however long would never be enough, he realized. He bent and crossed her mouth with his. Kissing her deeply, he savored her sweet flavor, a combination of tastes as exciting as spring in a mountain meadow and as seductive as a rich blend of Margolian chocolate.

Nicole sighed into his mouth and her fingers curled through his hair. *Safe.* Like the vines of the morning glory surrounding the cottage front porch, the feeling wound through her. The sensation blossomed with bright splashes of awareness. She'd never felt quite so secure as she did at this moment, held protectively in André's embrace. If all of this was a fantasy world, she hoped the clock would never strike midnight.

Breathless by the time André broke the kiss, she rested her head on his shoulder. She stood there, dreamily aware of the heavy beat of her heart and André's breath teasing the fine hair at her temple as she took in her new surroundings.

The cottage had a rustic, comfortable feel to it, making Nicole think of cozy winter nights sitting in front of the big stone fireplace. There'd be popcorn and spicy cider, warm fuzzy slippers ... and André. Romantic notions swirled through her imagination like a series of still photos slightly out of focus around the edges.

A bookcase crammed full and spilling its contents onto the floor drew her attention. "Who's the reader?" she asked.

"They were Christian's. I brought them from home."

Lifting her head, she shot him a puzzled look. "You're a secret reader?" Two books were open on an end table. The rest looked as if they'd been well thumbed.

With a frown tugging his brows together, he shoved his hands into his pockets. "I assume you will keep my secret?"

"Depends on what you've been reading." Curious, she strolled across the room and picked out a book at random—a treatise on economic reform in underdeveloped countries. The next one had to do with hydroelectric power, another on taxation policies.

Flipping through the pages, she said, "You're full of surprises. First I discover you're a natural when it comes to farming and mechanical things. And now I find you're an intellect at heart." She glanced across the room to André. "Why all this heavy reading?"

"I am asking the people of Margolis to trust me as their leader. I need to prepare myself."

"But you couldn't possibly have read all of this just since Christian died."

He settled his hips on the back of the couch and crossed his arms. "I'm working my way through them as best I can."

"My God, you've set yourself up for an enormous task."

"Damn it, Christian could handle it. So can I." A muscle rippled in his jaw.

"I don't doubt you, André. It's just—"

"That I'm a playboy."

"Don't say that. I believe you can be anything you want to be."

"He was the eldest and he cast a long shadow, even when we were children. I loved him . . ." Tense lines formed around his mouth and he visibly struggled with the weight of his memories. "In my father's eyes, I never quite measured up."

"You were younger. No one should have expected you to be a replica of your brother." She crossed the room to him and stood between his legs. As his arms slid around her waist and his hands gloved the curve of her hips, she felt a new upwelling of love. "I have the feeling you've made a career of hiding all your wonderful attributes."

One corner of his lips tilted into a wry smile. "Perhaps you are the only one who has taken the time to see them."

Given the option, Nicole would shout the news from the rooftops. "Now that you know Hendrik wasn't behind Christian's death, is the election any less important to you?''

His lips shifted into a determined line. "He is strangling the country. Nothing has altered that fact."

"Then you've got to let the people know who you really are. Don't hide yourself, André. Not the person you really are."

"What people believe, right or wrong, is hard to change. After years of playing one role, I cannot simply announce I was never really that person. They would not believe me." He pulled her closer against him, reaching around to cup her derriere so she could feel the hard ridge of his arousal. "As to my attributes . . . perhaps there is one that is of particular interest to you?"

"Oh? What did you have in mind?" she teased, willing to be distracted.

"I could demonstrate here on the couch, if you would like. Or perhaps on the rug in front of the fireplace."

The thrill of anticipation shot through her. She'd never be able to deny him anything he wanted. He was her heart, her life, her love. "I suppose we could start here and work our way to the bedroom."

"There are three bedrooms," he noted, his eyes darkening with desire. "There are also woods with quiet meadows, and grassy spots beside the creek. I think it will be necessary to explore all of our options quite thoroughly before we settle on any one locale.''

Her gaze slid with interest to the lush throw rug in front of the fireplace. "I am yours to command, *monsieur.*"

CONTENTMENT and fierce sexual satisfaction weighed André's limbs when he awoke from a sated nap sometime later. The slanted rays of sunlight cut a path through the window of the cottage. Clearly, the combination of terrific sex and an all-night drive had left him exhausted or he would not have fallen asleep on the floor. He could not even recall when Nicole had covered him with a soft wool blanket.

Slowly, he opened one eye.

Nicole had found one of his old velour robes, upstairs in the bedroom, he imagined. Barefoot, she was examining an old cuckoo clock on the knotty pine wall across the room. With her hair hanging loose to her shoulder blades, the blue robe reaching nearly to her ankles, and her tentative gestures, she looked like an eager child fighting the urge to touch a new toy. The sight brought a smile to André's lips.

"Do you like the clock?" he asked.

With a guilty start at the sound of his voice, she withdrew her hand. "I wasn't going to damage it."

He levered himself upright. "Of course not. Why would you think I would be worried about that?"

A flush colored her cheeks. "It's truly exquisite and I . . ." She gave him a sheepish smile. "Old habits die hard, I guess."

He found his clothes neatly stacked on the couch. As he pulled on his trousers, André raised questioning brows.

"My mother was the live-in housekeeper for a huge mansion in Beverly Hills, and we lived in a tiny apartment over the garage. As a rule, I wasn't allowed inside the big house. If I needed to talk to her, or if I was bleeding to death because of some tumble I'd taken, I had to stand outside the back door and *discreetly* call to her. The owner, you see, didn't much like children around."

"He does not sound like a very nice man."

"My mother thought he was." With a troubled frown, Nicole used her fingers to spear her hair back from her forehead. "Of course, the net result of my being forbidden *inside* the big house was to make it all the more desirable. So when he was away, and Mother wasn't looking, I'd sneak in."

"And sometimes you would get caught," he guessed, angry Nicole had been made to feel unwelcome no matter how sumptuous the house might have been.

"Not often." She shrugged. "I got pretty good about timing my excursions when everyone would be gone for a while. Then I'd walk through one spacious room after the other, staring at everything . . . the sterling-silver tea set, original oil paintings, beautiful furniture, fine porcelain figurines . . .'' Sighing, she crossed her arms at her waist and stuffed her hands into the opposite sleeves of the robe. "But I never touched a thing. I didn't dare. It might have cost Mother her job."

"But you wanted to."

"Like I was addicted," she admitted with a wry shake of her head.

André sensed how painful Nicole's childhood must have been, like living next door to a chocolate factory and being told she would never have a chance to taste that which was so temptingly close at hand. He did not envy her the experience.

"So you found yourself drawn to the antique business," he surmised.

"Actually, when I was fifteen I desperately wanted a job—any job—so I'd have some spending money of my own. I went everywhere I could think of and ended up polishing silver at an antique store after school every day." She grimaced. "There is, by the way, no more grungy job than that. But it's where I began to really learn about and appreciate fine things."

At least her love of antiques had led her to Margolis, André mused as he slipped his arm into his shirtsleeve. He tried to fight the nagging question that her attraction to expensive *things* might just as easily deceive her into believing she loved a man who could provide her with all the material goods she had obviously missed as a child.

Since he had never known poverty or even life as a member of the middle class, he could hardly blame her for desiring something better.

Still, a man needed to be loved for himself. Wealth, he had long since discovered, could be as much handicap as benefit when trying to discern a woman's true feelings.

FOR THE NEXT three days, Nicole discovered a whole new level of intimacy. She hadn't thought it possible to make love in so many different places, or in so many different ways. Totally isolated from the rest of the world, they had indulged themselves in an orgy of intimate exploration, broken only during the evening hours when André diligently studied his books.

During the days, fishing rarely held his interest for long, and she had yet to see so much as one much-touted native trout except as a quicksilver flash beneath a sheltered bank of a quiet pond. As far as she could tell, fish for eating still came from a grocery store.

Fortunately, the cottage had been well stocked with food. On the first afternoon, Sebastian had arrived with suitcases for each of them, then left as quickly as he'd come, leaving Nicole and André in their private world with enough changes of clothing to see them through a week or more.

As she lay on her back next to him on the grass, once again thoroughly sated, she watched the late afternoon sunlight catch a golden aspen leaf as it drifted slowly downward. A faint breeze caressed her bare flesh at the same time it twisted the leaf in mid-air, sending it off in a new direction. The nearby creek wound through the trees with a muted rush across a gravel bottom. From time to time, a dove added a soft cooing melody to the song of the forest, or a woodpecker contributed percussion notes.

At first Nicole had felt uncomfortable about making love out in the open, nervous someone might catch them in the act. Now it seemed the most natural thing in the world.

Knowing—and loving—André had changed her.

Reaching for her blouse, she suppressed a shiver of anxiety that good things always had to end.

As she turned away, he caught her hand.

"Did you hear it?" he asked.

"Hear what?" His muscular body lay fully exposed to her perusal and, in spite of herself, she never tired of studying the swirling pattern of his dark chest hair or the long, powerful length of his legs. What lay between those two spots held considerable fascination, too, she admitted, knowing she'd be able to look at André for the rest of her life and always find some new "attribute" to admire.

"A Gypsy violin. I had forgotten they camp nearby each autumn." He raised himself to one elbow. "They dance and tell each other's fortunes, I imagine."

She caught the plaintive strains of the violin then and was suddenly drawn to the sound. At some instinctive level, she fought the urge. Danger lurked in that direction. "Let's get back to the cottage." Hurriedly, she pulled her clothes on.

At a more leisurely pace, André tugged his jeans up his powerful legs. "I like to visit the Gypsies when they are here. It is said they bring good luck wherever they camp. And they are on my land."

"Maybe tomorrow," she urged. The sound of the music was too compelling, almost like an angels sounding to warn of impending doom.

Laughing, he snaked his arm around her waist and lifted her off the ground. "You do not have superstitious fears of Gypsy fortune-tellers, do you?"

"No, of course not." As he twirled her around, she clung to his shoulders. Desperately, she held on. "I'd just rather spend the time alone with you."

"Ah, my sweet little princess, I suggest only a small diversion. Then we shall return to our secluded cottage for a proper ending to a most pleasant day."

Without making a total fool of herself, Nicole couldn't think of any reason to argue. But deep in her heart she sensed the clock had just ticked—*one minute till midnight*.

THEY FOUND the Gypsies encamped in a huge meadow that stretched across both sides of the creek. A dozen motorized caravans and a couple of traditional horse-drawn wagons were parked in a circle. A thin trail of smoke rose from a smoldering camp fire, then drifted through the treetops. While people dressed in colorful costumes milled around the site visiting with friends, a solo harmonica joined the violin in a lazy tune.

"I am told before the Great War thousands of Gypsies camped here each year," André said. He linked his fingers through Nicole's as they walked down a gentle slope through summer-dry grass to the meadow. His jeans made a little swishing noise with each long-legged stride, sounds Nicole tried to memorize in case she never had another chance to hear them. "There are even those who claim King Stanislow used to visit this site."

"Why would he come here?" The hem of Nicole's denim skirt attracted drying grass seeds like a magnet.

"He had his own hunting lodge not far away, so the stories are probably true."

"If the king was so tight with the Gypsies, why were they driven out of the country?"

"I did not say Stanislow was friendly with them, only that he came here often. No doubt the women were beautiful... and accommodating. For that reason, he would set aside his personal prejudices and ignore those of his countrymen."

"Anything for an accommodating woman," she agreed, free-floating anxiety continuing to plague her. Men, the ruling class in particular, had few scruples when it came to how they used their women.

At least, that was what Nicole's mother had discovered.

Slanting André a glance, she hoped she wouldn't have to relearn the same lesson at painful personal expense.

Wandering into the encampment, they caught a few curious gazes and some that were not exactly friendly. An uncomfortable knot tightened in Nicole's stomach.

"André, let's not stay," she pleaded.

"We at least have to say hello to Petra," he responded, nodding toward the Gypsy woman when she appeared at the back of her caravan.

"Ah, our princess!" In a flurry of bright, swirling skirts and jingling bracelets, Petra rushed toward them. "I had hoped you would find your way."

Flustered by the woman's effusive welcome, Nicole stammered, "W-we're, ah, s-staying nearby for a few days."

"Yes, of course." Petra shifted her attention to André. "Your stars have been in ascendancy these recent days."

He grinned. "You mean, Hendrik is having trouble with the press?"

She joined him with a mirthful smile. "The media has not held up a kind mirror for the prime minister."

"André thought it would be better if we stayed out of sight for a while," Nicole said.

"Your secret is safe with us, Princess." Her dark eyes gleaming with mischief, Petra took Nicole's arm. "Come, you must meet all of our people. They will want you to dance for them tonight. With your handsome *gaje,* of course."

"But I—"

Try as she might, objecting proved quite useless as Nicole was swept along by the tidal wave of Petra's enthusiasm. She met the violin player, a man with far more wrinkles creasing his face than strings on his instrument, and visited with his daughter, who had two grandchildren playing at her feet. At the urging of a cluster of men, André vanished to watch a horse race.

Nicole felt suddenly alone in a crowd. And at the same time she had the oddest sense of...coming home. A feeling she resisted. She had no connection with these people. None.

Her undefined panic surged with each swooping strain of the violin.

The rich scent of roasting pig filled the air. There was laughter and the occasional heartfelt tear as new arrivals appeared and old friends met after a year of separation.

"Come, little one," Petra insisted as the sun dipped behind a hill. "You must get ready for the evening's festivities."

"I really can't stay. I have to find André." *He'll take me back to where I am safe,* she thought irrationally.

"Trust me, Princess. Your *gaje* will find you, just as the old king found your grandmother."

"No!" Filled with angry denial, Nicole yanked her arm free of Petra's grasp. "I don't know what you're talking about."

"There is nothing for you to fear, my child."

Nicole felt reality—the truth she'd never wanted to face—tighten around her chest. "Please, I don't want to—"

"I was only a child when your grandmother fled our homeland, and I recall her only as a beautiful young woman whom I admired. A lovely Gypsy princess. She left something for you with my mother—for the child she carried in her belly, or the child who would follow—in case you ever found your way home."

Nicole stifled another groan of denial as she entered Petra's dimly lit wagon. The close quarters carried the residual scent of a kerosene lamp and bedding not yet aired. As Petra sat on the edge of the bed, her silver bracelets jingled, causing Nicole to experience a dizzying sense of déjà vu—a sound so familiar in her youth.

"Did your grandmother not tell you of your family?" Petra asked.

Nicole shook her head. "It was so long ago. She may have, but I was too young." And her mother had not welcomed stories of the Old Country. She wanted to be an *American*.

Patting the rumpled bed clothes, Petra invited Nicole to sit. "We are a proud people, my child. While kings have come and gone, we Gypsies have survived. It is time you learn of your history."

As Petra began the tale, Nicole listened reluctantly, then little by little she was drawn into the story of a people's survival against centuries of prejudice. And their pride. Always a feeling of pride.

Though the shadows had deepened, Nicole wasn't sure how much time had passed when Petra announced, "You need not feel shame for your ancestry, or for the sake of your grandmother. She loved the old king, whose seed she carried from this land, and he loved her. For a Gypsy woman that is enough."

Nicole felt tears thicken in her throat. Like her grandmother before her, André's love would be enough if she could lay claim to it. "Thank you," she whispered. "Thank you for giving me back my history, my pride."

With a shrug, Petra dismissed her gratitude. "Now we must prepare for the dance."

"I don't know how to do Gypsy dances," she protested.

"Bah. I have just spent hours telling you of your past. Our dances are in your blood, Princess. They are a part of your soul. Do you not feel them?"

Oddly, Nicole did feel a new beat pulsing through her veins. A Gypsy rhythm? she wondered. Perhaps she had simply never listened to her own instincts before with such clear understanding.

"Tonight, my little princess..." Petra lifted the lid on an old wooden trunk. "Tonight you will dance for your *gaje* as your grandmother danced for hers, and Montiard will learn what it is to love a Gypsy." Petra slipped four silver bracelets onto Nicole's arm, a loving legacy from her grandmother.

ANDRÉ TIPPED the bottle to his lips again. The clear liquid burned down his throat all the way to his belly, though not as painfully as the first time. Or the second.

"Gypsies must have stomachs coated with iron," he complained, his eyes watering.

One of his companions, a swarthy fellow built with the shoulders and arms of a circus strongman, took the bottle from him and downed a swig. "For a *gaje*, you appear able to hold your own."

"Frankly, I much prefer the products of Margolis vineyards." He also wished he knew where Nicole had gone. Darkness had settled on the encampment and he had not seen her since she went off with Petra. The musicians had arranged themselves on one side of the blazing fire. With a frown, he noted only men were lounging around the clearing. "Where did all the women go?"

"They have been preparing for the dance. Soon now, my impatient friend, your princess will rejoin you."

A moment later, when the stars appeared at their brightest and the flames from the fire settled into a flickering orange glow, the violin began the strains of a haunting melody. The music wafted sensuously around the clearing. Beckoning, each stroke of the bow an invitation. As other instruments created new harmonies, André felt the pull of the chords vibrating deep in his loins.

He became aware of women walking out of the shadows toward the fire, arriving singly or in pairs. Of every age, they circled, their hips swaying with each rhythmic step, their full skirts making a sibilant sound to match the music. A hundred silver bracelets worn on graceful arms echoed the beat, and castanets softly thrummed. Firelight glistened off of creamy flesh exposed by low-cut blouses.

A sheen of sweat dampened André's forehead. Staring at the moving silhouettes, he strained to identify Nicole—his princess—among the women.

Air lodged in his throat at the moment of recognition.

Her hair hung loosely down her back, shifting across her shoulders in a gilded cascade of golds and reds. Light and shadow alternately emphasized the curve of her breasts, the slender width of her waist and the full shape of her enticing hips. Bracelets glittered on her arms. She moved with the same natural grace as a ballerina, born to the steps of a Gypsy dance.

It took all of André's willpower not to leap to his feet and drag her off into the woods to claim her, heart and soul, for himself. No other man had the right to see her in so sensual a way. She was his alone. Forever.

The ferocity of the emotion stunned him. It was as though Nicole had ripped open his chest and bared his heart to feelings he had spent a lifetime avoiding. He felt helpless in the face of such terrible vulnerability.

She swayed toward him. Silhouetted against the fire, she was both fallen angel and virginal princess, a combination of all the traits that create a perfect woman. Looping a vibrant red silk scarf around the back of his neck, she urged him to his feet.

"Will you do the steps with me?" she asked in provocative invitation. Her eyes were wide, questioning him in a guileless way that held both fear and anticipation.

His throat constricted. "I am not sure I know them."

"Perhaps we will learn together."

Linked by the softness of silk, she taught him the pleasure of slow, measured rhythms, and long, gliding movements. At first hesitantly, then with a greater sense of confidence, they followed the metered steps. The music wove a magic spell around them that cast out any other thought. They were alone in the golden glow of the fire, beneath a sky filled with sparkling diamonds. The velvet night caressed them. Feet and torsos moved in instinctive, matching response to ancient urges conjured by the bittersweet strains of the melody.

Subtly, the beat altered, accelerating dips and turns, bringing their bodies closer together. Castanets clicked with increasing urgency. Through the fullness of skirts and the thickness of jeans, thighs brushed. Hands sighed over aching flesh. Sparks from the fire danced into the dark sky.

The scent of wood smoke filled the air. And the sweet, seductive fragrance of passion.

This was more than mere sexual enticement, André realized. It was a dance of commitment, a mingling of two souls that had found each other. A marriage witnessed by the stars and the rising fullness of the moon.

He didn't know when the music stopped. Or even if it had. He simply knew he had to acknowledge his new awareness in the only way possible.

He led Nicole away from the fire, away from the Gypsy encampment, to a secluded spot sheltered by large granite outcroppings and carpeted with grass. The autumn scent of fading wildflowers enveloped the glade. In awe, he lay down beside her.

With exquisite care for the gift she had given him, André worshiped Nicole. With his lips and hands, with his soul, he paid homage to the beautiful woman who had once said she loved him. Only once. But that was a beginning. He would coax those words from her again and again.

Her soft cries of pleasure affirmed his commitment; at her passionate response, he redoubled his efforts to please. She claimed him, changed him, and he was helpless to resist. Nor did he want to. He would have pledged his love through all eternity, but his throat was clogged with the wonder of rebirth.

Sighing, she brought his head to rest at the fragrant crook of her neck, and he gave himself over to the contented sense of floating on a cushion of sensuous clouds.

THE FEELING of contented revelation stayed with André even as they skirted the Gypsy camp the following morning and made their way, hand-in-hand, back to Dove's Roost.

The sight of Sebastian's old Volvo parked in front of the cottage jarred him. He wasn't yet ready to face the intrusion of reality.

His friend burst out of the front door. "Where in damnation have you been?"

André shrugged noncommittally. "Avoiding the press, as we discussed."

Sebastian's expression torqued into one of total exasperation and he released a sigh. His gray suit was thoroughly rumpled, as though he had slept in it, and his paisley tie was all askew. "My friend, we are in deep trouble."

His campaign manager cut a worried look at Nicole. "We may well have made a serious tactical error."

Chapter Twelve

She'd known it was coming. Perhaps since the moment Petra had read her palm at the antique store, Nicole had realized the dark, secretive truth her mother had spent a lifetime denying would change Nicole's future course. And very likely cost her the man she loved. The realization carried with it such enormous pain, she felt dizzy. A wave a nausea swept over her, and she brought her hand to her throat.

"What is the problem?" André asked his campaign manager in a tone that evidenced his displeasure. "Is Hendrik attacking me again?"

"He does not have to. Our friend, Robert von Helman, has provided all the ammunition necessary to destroy your campaign without Hendrik having to raise another finger."

"Robert has done that?" With a good deal of impatience, André speared his fingers through his dark hair. "Tell me what has happened."

"His newspaper associates have finally traced the immigration records in the States, and he confirmed the report with his sources in Paris." Sebastian slid Nicole another troubled look. "I am afraid Robert discovered your wife is *not* the heir to the Margolis throne. In fact," he lowered his voice, "her ancestors were... *Gypsies.*"

Nicole held her breath while André absorbed Sebastian's pronouncement. He would send her away, she was sure. She watched as varied emotions crossed his face in rapid succession—surprise, shocked denial. Finally his aristocratic features settled into a dark twist of anger.

"That is a lie! She carries the mark of Margolis."

Sebastian shrugged. "I cannot explain that, my friend. Perhaps it is nothing more than coincidence. I know only what Robert has reported appears to have considerable basis in fact."

"What the hell kind of loyalty is that? I thought he was one of my supporters."

When André's fingers flexed into fists, Nicole laid a restraining hand on his arm. Her gesture set off the soft jingle of the silver bracelets she wore and her heart constricted. *Gypsy music.* The loving sound of her grandmother. How could she have forgotten so easily? "I can explain how I came to have the mark on my neck," she admitted.

His gaze snapped around to meet hers. "You are a princess. Any fool can see that. Even the dottering old monarchists wanted to claim you as their ruler."

"They will not want that now," Sebastian warned.

"What Robert discovered is the truth," Nicole said as calmly as she could, though her heart beat heavily against her ribs. "My grandmother was a Gypsy." She lifted her chin a little at the admission.

André stared at her. "You cannot be so sure."

"I should have put the pieces together years ago, but I was only a little girl when my grandmother died." Because she simply could not resist, Nicole touched her fingertips to André's whisker-roughened cheek. He was so masculine, so ruggedly virile. "My grandmother, who was a *Gypsy* princess, was King Stanislow's mistress when she was a very young woman. When he was assassinated, she fled the country, as did many other Gypsies. At the time, she was pregnant with my mother."

"That explains the use of LeDeaux as a last name," Sebastian pointed out. "It is reasonable a pregnant woman would want to claim the benefit of marriage."

"Maybe they *were* married," André suggested, a muscle rippling in his jaw. "That would make Nicole the legal heir and nothing has changed. The ceremony could have been performed in secret."

"No, it wasn't," Nicole said simply. "My mother spent her whole life trying to deny, even to herself, that she was both a Gypsy and illegitimate. I think it must have nearly killed her when she got pregnant with me, and my father wouldn't marry her. The experience made her more bitter than I had realized.

And lying about the past made her a miserable person. From now on, there'll be no more lies. None. No matter what the cost." Even if it brought heartache, Nicole vowed she'd face life with her chin held high. She was, after all, descended from a long line of proud people. Her only concern was that her past not adversely affect André.

He caught her hand, bringing her palm to his lips for a quick kiss. "The people will still think of you as their princess. They already love you. How could they not?"

"You've told me yourself how deep prejudices are against the Gypsies in Margolis. They may not be willing to accept me."

Clearing his throat, Sebastian said, "She is right, André. The public will never tolerate a Gypsy as the wife of the prime minister. Perhaps as a mistress . . ."

His hurtful words brought the press of tears to the backs of Nicole's eyes. She'd dreamed of so much more, even when she'd doubted the possibility.

André whirled on his friend. "Then I will not be the damn prime minister!" he bellowed. His shout startled a flock of doves from their perches and the air filled momentarily with a shower of white feathers. "Nicole is my wife and she is going to stay that way."

Squeezing her eyes shut, Nicole realized she would never allow herself to be the cause of André giving up his goal. Being prime minister was too important to him; and his success in the election was crucial to the future of the country. She was absolutely convinced of that. If she stayed, she might destroy him, along with all of his dreams. And whatever he felt for her now would turn to bitterness and hate. She'd never risk that.

"No." The thickness in her throat made the word come out in a barely audible whisper. "You've forgotten our arrangement, André. A marriage of convenience. Remember? Obviously our relationship is no longer convenient for you. Instead I've become a burden and potentially damaging to your candidacy. Besides..." This was the hard part, the last lie she would ever tell. "I have to get home...to America. I have a business to start."

Black fury darkened his expression. He caught her chin between his thumb and forefinger, forcing her to look him in the eye. "Your lies are always too transparent, my love. You owe me one more week of your time. *That* was part of the bargain. A full two months. And I intend to claim every moment."

"You don't understand. I don't belong here. I never have—"

He silenced her with a kiss. She struggled against his overwhelming determination and the drugging desire that flared through her. For his sake, and that of the country, she had to remember her place.

ON THE HURRIED DRIVE back to the House of Montiard they shared little conversation. André had never been in such a black mood. He knew Sebastian was very likely right, and hated the messenger who had delivered the news. His marriage to Nicole could well cost him the election. He railed at the unfairness of it all. Prejudice sapped energy that could be better used to enhance the country's economy. Without Nicole at his side, the entire effort seemed suddenly meaningless.

He slanted her a glance. With her shoulders hunched forward and her hair forming an auburn veil that hid her face, she had withdrawn into herself. He could almost see her considering her options. All too easily she had announced her plan to return to the States. Her proposal had very nearly shattered him.

After all they had had together, did he mean so little to her? As little as he had meant to the mother who had deserted him?

Doubts assailing him, André sped past a contingent of the press corps at the entrance to the estate and wheeled up the long drive to the house, vowing he would not let her go. She had taught him too much.

When the car pulled to a stop, Nicole looked up. She etched into her memory every line of the dramatic portico and its symmetrical columns. A hilltop castle that had briefly been her home.

The front door flew open and Madame Montiard appeared, her dachshunds spilling out of the house in a flurry of wagging tails. Nicole smiled at their energy as she tried to keep from stepping on them.

"My dear child," André's grandmother cried, "they are saying such terrible things about you." She gave Nicole a fierce hug that belied her tiny stature. "Dreadful accusations. Meier-Wahl is behind it all, of course. Nothing more than politics as usual. We will fight him, you know. We cannot allow him to drag the Montiard name through the mud and slander—"

"Madame," Nicole said softly, but with a good deal of intensity, "the reports are true. My grandmother was a Gypsy princess and mistress to the king."

"Ridiculous, my dear. The old king would not have consorted with those people. No, no. He simply would not have done such a thing. And certainly my grandson would not have married—"

"*Grand-mère*, be careful what you say," André warned.

She waved off André's words and the possibility of Nicole being a Gypsy—a possibility she could never accept—with her cane as if it were a magic wand. "Now, my children, we must make our plans. Another party, I think. Something quite grand. Perhaps we might even invite some lesser personages this time. Perhaps a duke or earl from England. I once met this lovely woman who had known the czar. Royalty of some sort, as I recall. I will look her up in my files." Still talking, more to herself than to Nicole, she turned to enter the house, the dogs at her heels. "If Charles is available, he might drop by. Pity about Di . . ."

Heartsick, Nicole said to André, "I'm sorry. I wanted her to understand. To face the truth." If his grandmother could know her and still not welcome her as a Gypsy, how could Nicole expect anyone in the country to do so?

"I fear *Grand-mère* has lived her own kind of truth for many years. She is unlikely to change at this late date." He slid his hand beneath Nicole's hair and massaged the back of her neck with his talented fingers.

"You're not very good about facing facts, either, André. In terms of your campaign, marrying me was a mistake."

His fingers closed with a quiet sense of desperation around her flesh. "I will not believe that. Not yet. Together we will take our case to the people. They loved you once. They will again."

"And if they don't?"

He hesitated a fractional beat, just long enough for Nicole to know the emotional torment he was experiencing. He might very well love her, though he'd never spoken the words, but he wasn't ready to give up his chance to be prime minister for her. And how could she blame him?

"Give me time to prove they will," he pleaded. "A few days. That is all I ask."

Slowly, she nodded her agreement. The next few days would set the course for her entire future. She felt as though her happiness rode on every breath she took.

USING OVERSIZE SCISSORS, Nicole snipped the wide ribbon to officially open the new children's wing at the San Margo Hospital. Among the sparse crowd of onlookers, there was only scattered applause. A single flashbulb popped. The much-touted event hadn't even attracted the press corps in significant numbers. Nothing she and André had done in the past three days had managed to counter accusations that her claims to the throne had been a hoax from the beginning. Just another Gypsy trick, they claimed. She'd been labeled an impostor, and André had been painted with the same dirty brush. His popularity had plummeted. Hendrik, no doubt, was gloating.

In spite of a heavy heart, Nicole forced a smile and knelt to accept an armful of flowers from a girl of about six. The vibrant blooms contrasted starkly with Nicole's mood. Time was running out.

"Hi, sweetheart," she said. "What's your name?"

"Miriam," came the shy response.

Nicole smoothed her hand over the child's dark, silken hair—hair finer than André's but blessed with the same characteristic waves. "You're a very pretty girl, Miriam, and your flowers are lovely. Thank you very much."

Her wide, brown eyes studied Nicole. "Mama says the bad people will not let you be princess anymore."

"I guess I wasn't ever *really* a princess, honey, at least, not the kind they expected me to be. But I didn't know that." The press had made it abundantly clear being a Gypsy princess didn't count.

"Mama thinks it is not fair. She says anybody ought to be a princess if they want to."

"Well, you thank your mother for me, but I'm sure she knows that sometimes life isn't fair." Smiling past the threat of tears, she placed a soft kiss on the top of the child's head. Very soon now her fantasy would be over... her carriage would turn into a pumpkin and her handsome prince would appear only in her dreams. She felt the inevitability as surely as someone can feel the rumble of an approaching avalanche.

She had to face that truth and move on to the rest of her life. She was a housekeeper's daughter—part Gypsy, part bastard of royalty—a survivor, a woman who had scrimped and saved to start her own business. She *would* succeed. No one died of a broken heart. It just felt that way.

Standing, she glanced toward André. With determined friendliness, he shook hands with each of the few visitors. The women smiled up at him with considerable admiration; the men more often scowled. All the time, André looked tall and proud, and she knew he was losing the battle for votes.

The pompous hospital director rudely pushed his way between André and the man he was speaking with. "Come along, now. We must keep on schedule. Everyone is to take the tour of the facility. We have a state-of-the-art surgery, but scaled down to size so as to not frighten our wee ones." Blatantly ignoring André, he ushered the rest of the group toward the hallway like a teacher herds recalcitrant students. "And in the playroom you will find . . ."

His voice faded away, and the visitors with him, leaving André and Nicole alone in the waiting area. Despair washed over her. She'd done this to him, brought his campaign to its knees when he should have been riding on a wave of popular support.

What was he thinking? she wondered. Did he feel regret for how all of this had started? And would he be sad, at least for a little while, when their time together was over? For surely he must realize by now that his only chance at winning the election would be for her to leave.

He extended his hand to her. "Do you know what really galls me?"

She interlinked her fingers through his, loving the feel of his warm, callused palm, his strength that he so often hid behind an easygoing veneer. "What?"

"I contributed the money to build this damn wing. Every bloody franc. Anonymously. Now that asinine director acts as if I am a leper."

"He's a government employee, which means he probably owes his job to Hendrik. Besides, if you gave the money, why didn't you insist this part of the hospital be named after you? The Montiard Children's Wing, or something? That would have been good politics.''

''No, they would have said I was trying to *buy* votes. And the fact is, a lot of our children have had to go out of the country when they became seriously ill because we lacked the necessary facilities to treat them. Now they can stay closer to home, near their parents. That was the reason for the contribution. Not politics.''

A band of love tightened around her chest and she squeezed his hand. ''Has anyone told you lately that you're a really nice guy?''

''Not lately,'' he conceded with a wry grin that nearly brought tears to her eyes.

When they returned to the House of Montiard, Sebastian was waiting for André. The two men closeted themselves away the rest of the afternoon and it was long after dinner before Nicole could corner the campaign manager alone.

''I want to know the truth,'' she began. ''How is the campaign going?''

In an automatic gesture, Sebastian brushed his blond hair back from his forehead. ''Not well. André has lost ten points in the polls just this week and many of the party's candidates are slipping almost as badly.''

''Because of me?''

"I am sorry, Nicole. In many ways, this debacle is my fault. I should have thought before I suggested—"

"There's no need for you to take all the blame. The fact is, we both want André to win. So what can we do? What can I do?" Desperately, she wanted Sebastian to come up with an alternative that would allow her to stay.

Heaving a sigh, he crossed his arms and leaned back against the elegant *secrétaire* in the reception room where she'd finally caught him alone. Lights from the chandelier cast shadows across the face of a troubled man. "If I knew the answer to that question, I assure you I would have already told André. With only two days until the election, the situation looks bleak."

"Yes." Her throat felt so tight, speaking even a single word rasped across every nerve. "If...if I left André? Would that help him?"

The implication of her question leveled his eyebrows. "If I could announce André was divorcing you, because he now realizes you lied to him..." He considered the idea. "Yes, I believe that would improve his position. But even that would not guarantee his election."

Her chin quivered. "Can you get me out of the country without anyone knowing?"

"Tonight?"

"No!" she said too quickly. She couldn't leave yet. *Please God*, not before she had a chance to say goodbye in her own way. "In the morning?"

"Nicole, are you sure you wish to do this? Your leaving may help the campaign, but what about André's feelings? You should at least consult with—"

"I won't let either you or André stop me." Feeling her courage falter as tears threatened, she renewed her resolve. "If you don't help me, I'll find another way to leave."

"As you wish, *mademoiselle*." He lifted his shoulders in resigned agreement. "There is an early flight to Paris. I know enough people that I could slip you on board under a false name. But how would I get you out of the house without André seeing you leave? And asking a great many questions?"

"You leave André to me. Just meet me before dawn on the road at the bottom of the hill. Later you can—" she swallowed hard "—tell André I thought this was for the best."

"Are you sure about this, Nicole?" His eyes filled with concern, though she couldn't tell if it was for her or for the campaign. "The polls could be wrong."

"Don't you think that's too big a gamble to take?"

He dipped his head in a respectful bow. "As you wish, *mademoiselle*."

Turning before he could see the tears spilling down her cheeks, she hurried from the room.

EVEN KNOWING André was waiting for her, Nicole took extra care preparing for bed—her last night with the man she would always love. She hadn't given her heart easily. Others might think it had all happened too fast, but she'd been aware, almost from the beginning, that André was a man of great depth and empathy. She'd seen it in the way he treated his grandmother, and cared about Jean Paul and his wife. How the farmers loved him. A woman could have done worse in choosing a prince to sweep her off her feet.

She slicked a fragrant bath oil over her arms and legs and across her breasts, remembering how André's tapered fingers felt caressing her heated flesh. The tactile memory was so strong, she knew she would never forget his touch. Not if she lived to be a hundred.

Like a cloud of silk, her negligee slipped over her head in a whisper of sheer fabric.

Picking up the chilled bottle of champagne and tray with two crystal glasses, she carried them from the dressing room. Her pulse beat heavy strokes in her throat.

Since their return from the mountains, they'd chosen to sleep in André's room with its heavy, masculine furniture and massive four-poster. She imagined the combination of dark wood and the scent of rich oil polish would always trigger erotic images in Nicole's mind . . . visions she would cherish.

When she found him, he was already in bed, one arm sprawled across her pillow. Her heart constricted at the sight of him. Bare from the waist up, his broad chest rose and fell with each easy breath. She admired the ridged hardness of his belly, the corded strength of his pectorals, and the breadth of his shoulders. Evening whiskers darkened his firm jaw. He gave her a sleepy, hooded look, and a smile played at the corners of his sensuous lips.

"What took you so long?" His low, intimate question spread over her awareness like a warm mist.

"I want tonight to be special for you."

He lifted his eyebrows in a slow question.

"You've been spending the last few weeks teaching me about making love." He'd given her so many wonderful memories, she wanted to return the favor. Or perhaps she simply wanted to be sure his recollections would be as clear as hers. "I thought tonight I'd show you what I've learned."

"Hmm. Sounds interesting." He folded back the corner of the blanket on her side of the bed. "Does that mean you're going to be on top?"

She felt a blush stain her cheeks as, for the moment, she declined his invitation to join him. Instead she moved to his side of the bed, placing the champagne bottle and tray of glasses beneath the single lamp on the nightstand. She'd never been the aggressor before. The thought was both exciting and titillating. "Being on top is among the activities I have in mind," she confided, her emotions lowering her voice to a sultry whisper.

His gaze never left her as she poured the champagne.

When he accepted the glass, he said, "This is definitely a good beginning."

"To the next prime minister of Margolis." She held her glass up for the bittersweet toast.

"To us," he countered.

The two crystal goblets came together in a clear, pure note, and she remembered the first time they had saluted their marriage. Now they were saying goodbye.

She swallowed a sip of champagne along with the tears that clogged her throat. Later there would be time to cry. But not now. Not when she wanted them both to remember this last night of passion with such joy.

As she watched André drink again from his glass, she began to slowly remove her nightgown. She slid it from her shoulders, then edged the fabric to the point where her nipples where just barely hidden. His eyes darkened with keen sexual awareness and he licked his lips.

"Princess, are you sure you know what you are doing to me?"

Noting the telltale evidence of his arousal beneath the light blanket, she smiled. "You'll tell me, won't you, if I do anything wrong?" She allowed the silk to slide to her hips. It gave her a sense of power to realize she could affect André with her newly acquired sensuality.

"If you keep up that striptease act much longer, I will not be able to speak at all." Once naked, she took the silk garment she had removed and dragged the fabric leisurely across his chest. His muscles rippled in waves, and she felt a responding clenching deep between her thighs.

With a low moan that was an agonizing mix of pleasure and frustration, André fisted the gown. In a surprise move, he dragged her down onto the bed beside him. "God, Nicole, are you trying to drive me mad?"

"Only temporarily," she assured him.

He caught the teasing gleam in her eyes. Never before had he seen her like this—lusty and carnal. Her hedonistic enthusiasm fired his own sexual engine, making his body hum like a high-powered machine that would all too soon spin out of control. Her slender fingers fluttering across his chest set off fiery sparks that nearly exploded his composure.

"No," she complained, refusing with a twist of her head the kiss he demanded. "Not yet." Dipping two fingers into her glass of champagne on the nightstand, she drew circles through the hair on his chest, dabbing an extra measure on each of his nipples.

"Nicole?" In spite of the chilled liquid, heat flared everywhere she touched.

"First I want to get drunk on you."

She bent her head, sending a cascade of floral-scented hair over his chest. He felt each separate auburn strand as though it were an erotic whip flaying him with incredible desire. The tip of her tongue teased at his flesh in heated strokes like a delicate cat licking milk from a saucer. Her teeth clenched gently over one nipple.

André's breath lodged in his lungs. "Where the hell did you learn that?"

Her throaty laugh was as sensual as the heat in his loins. "From you, my love. Where else?"

When Nicole dipped her fingers into the champagne again, then swirled them lower on his body, a new thrill coursed through her. She had no idea how much gratification she would receive in giving André pleasure. She made murmuring sounds as she tasted him, absorbing the heady flavor of champagne combined with his musky, male base note. She lost herself in his textures, the rough weave of curls across his chest and abdomen, the velvety tip of his manhood. He was drawn tight and hard, and she relished the thought of how thoroughly he would fill her. She kissed the muscular curve of his thigh—

"Enough!" André cried. Provoked beyond enduring, he slid his hand between her thighs. Finding her ready, he lifted her at the waist and gently entered her in a single stroke that left them both breathless. "Enough torture," he growled more roughly than he had intended. Never had he more clearly felt his power as a man. Nor his vulnerability. The dichotomy ripped at the foundations of his understanding. How could a woman make him feel so needy and omnipotent at the same time? The experience was so violently exciting, it humbled him.

Relenting, Nicole covered his lips with hers. She plunged her tongue wantonly into the warm velvet of his mouth—champagne-flavored, hot and wanting. His breath filled her lungs as his erect member invaded her welcoming body. They were one. Like the entwining threads of gold and silver on the most beautifully crafted piece of decorative art, there was no beginning, no end, only perfection.

She cried aloud at the glory of the moment as her body convulsed around him and she felt the shattering impact of his release.

When her heart and breathing had settled into a more easy rhythm, she dozed, her body still resting on top of him, his torpid manhood quiet within her. Later, he took her again. His way. Rising above her to spread her legs for a moist, slick entry to her womb.

Still, in the dark of the night, she forced herself to leave the warmth of his embrace. She was a far different person than the woman who had first arrived at the House of Montiard. Her innocence had been taken and in its place she had found pride in her past, an unexpected measure of strength. And she had learned about love, a passionate love for a man. Now she must accept the ultimate test of that emotion.

Could she truly give up that which she coveted beyond all else?

Dressing quickly, she fought the sense of dread that threatened her resolve. She took only her passport and the silver bracelets Petra had given her. The memories of André she would hold in her heart.

Escaping out the back of the house, she scurried down the weed-encrusted embankment to Sebastian's waiting car. Raindrops falling from a lowering sky disguised the tears that dampened her cheeks.

Chapter Thirteen

"What do you mean, she is gone?" The news sliced through André's gut with breathtaking force. Disbelief warred with his greatest fear, and he fought for control. Outside, the sky was as dark as his mood. Wind lashed rain against the windows in an angry downpour that swept across the top of the hill and veiled the orchards in the valley below the House of Montiard.

Sebastian shrugged. "I took her to the airport early this morning."

A muscle rippled in his jaw and he clenched his hands into fists. "Why in the name of God did you do that?"

"It was her idea, André."

"H-her idea?" he sputtered. "You did not have to go along with her scheme."

"I did not think you would care all that much. She is hardly the first woman in your life, nor is she likely to be the last. With her gone, the election—"

André grabbed his friend by his shirt collar and knotted it tight against his throat. "I do not give a damn about the election."

Sebastian paled. "She agreed to a divorce."

After all was said and done, Nicole had betrayed him. *As cruelly as his mother had betrayed his father.* "Divorce or not, I will not give her a single franc. Did you tell her that?" He ground out the words from between clenched teeth. How could she have duped him so easily? Last night he had been sure she would stay to face the verdict of the populace. And now she was gone.

Already an empty place was forming in his chest and he mentally wrapped a shield of steel around the hurt, just as he had when his mother had left.

"I supposed you let her clean me out," André accused. "Let her take everything of value that was not nailed down."

"She had only her purse, André. There was no time—"

"Do not lie to me, Sebastian. I know what women do when they tire of their husbands."

The sound of dachshunds running across tile floors announced the arrival of André's grandmother.

"Boys, boys! What is all this arguing about?" Dressed in a lavender morning coat, Madame Montiard flitted about the dining room.

"Nicole has left me," André said grimly.

"Nonsense. Such a nice girl. She would not leave us when the party is scheduled. So many plans to make. Charles is checking his calendar—"

"Grand-mère, she wants a divorce."

Her hands stilled in the act of pouring her coffee. The dark liquid filled the fragile china cup and spilled over the edge into the saucer.

Slowly, she set the pot down and raised her gaze to meet André's. "Did you drive her off?"

Feeling like a child about to be reprimanded, he stuffed his hands into his pockets. "Not likely."

"Then you must go after her and bring her back."

"She made her choice."

"You, my dear, young man, have the same stubborn pride that was your father's downfall. If he had asked your mother to return when she'd first left, she would have. But no, my son was too proud. Instead of telling her that he loved her, and you boys needed her, he cut your mother off from all contact."

André's forehead tightened into a frown. "Father always told us Mother had been the one to make the choice. She had only wanted his money." Giving in to monetary demands from his *former* wife was a mistake André would not repeat.

"She never kept a single franc he sent her. Not a sou. I think that angered him all the more. That and the letters she wrote to you boys, which your father destroyed without so much as opening them."

André felt a disorienting sensation deep inside him. *His father had lied to him.* And, by omission, his grandmother had, too. And now Nicole had left, taking nothing but the clothes on her back. None of this made sense. "Mother wrote to us?" The words made his throat feel raw with remembered pain.

"Oh, yes. Often at first, and then less frequently. I wanted to write her back, of course. It was the courteous thing to do." She twisted her hands together. "But your father forbade me."

André was struck by all those years he had wasted his anger on his mother, when others were at fault. Slowly the shield he had just put back in place developed a web of cracks.

"Why did you not tell me?" he asked.

"When you and Christian were little, I tried. But you believed your father. I thought it best not to interfere further."

"Dear God, I wish you had." Sighing, he shot Sebastian a questioning look.

"Nicole tried to hide it, my friend, but this morning she was crying. It is possible her talk of divorce was only meant as a way to aid your election, and did not come from her heart."

Hope flickered in André's chest. It might just be possible he could—

"With this storm," Sebastian continued, sensing after so many years of friendship the direction of André's thoughts, "it is possible all of the planes have been grounded. There might still be time."

"I will take the time," André vowed. "If I have to follow her all the way to the States, I will bring my wife back here where she belongs."

He gave Sebastian a few quick, very firm orders, then headed out the door.

THE THREE-HOUR flight delay had done little to bolster Nicole's spirits. When the airline personnel had finally announced boarding, she'd taken her seat on the aisle. That way she wouldn't have to endure watching the last speck of Margolis slip out of sight beneath the plane.

She noticed the man seated in front of her had dark, wavy hair. But it wasn't the *right* hair, strands so silken they wrapped themselves around her fingers when she curled her hands into their rich texture. By the window, the business traveler had long legs that barely fit in the close confines of tourist class at the back of the plane. But they were not the solid thighs, muscled by hard work, she wanted to touch.

"Princess."

She heard the name as part of the humming of air-conditioning vents and the whine of motors, so she didn't look up. Only her imagination, she chided herself. Only the longing within her that would always want to hear *his* voice calling her. If only he had said "I love you," her sacrifice would have been more bearable.

When she reached for the in-flight magazine, her focus blurring, she heard it again, more urgent this time than the first.

"Nicole!"

The plane shuddered as though anxious to be free of its earthly tether.

"Please, *monsieur,* you cannot come aboard without a ticket," a woman argued.

"Hold the plane, damn it!"

Nicole's gaze snapped up. The whir of motors roared like white noise through her head. Her heart accelerated until she thought it might take flight on its own.

He was striding down the aisle, his hair wind-blown and damp from the rain, with a single, be-draggled lock curled across his forehead, and she knew that even in the rain he hadn't bothered to put the top up on the car. His jaw was set at a determined angle. His eyes narrowed, he looked darkly down each row of seats. She had never seen him so compellingly handsome, so thoroughly in control, and she wasn't quite sure why he was there. Surely he realized . . .

When she saw he carried a small bouquet of violets, her pulse expanded, filling every nerve in her body with a rush of excited adrenaline.

He stopped beside her seat. "Come with me, Princess." His voice was low and raspy, unfairly intimate as it always was when he looked at her with those dark, sensual eyes.

"André…" His name caught in her throat. "You know I can't. The election—"

"You are my wife! Win or lose, your place is at my side."

"Think of what you'd be giving up. Your dreams. The future of your country."

"If my countrymen cannot accept you as my wife, Princess, then they deserve Hendrik."

A middle-aged woman seated across the aisle said, "Good for you, Monsieur Montiard. You have my vote."

Nicole flushed. She'd forgotten they were making a public spectacle of themselves. The news of this little scene would be spread across the whole continent as soon as the plane touched down in Paris.

A uniformed man with stripes on his sleeve strode down the aisle from the forward cabin. "*Monsieur*, I must ask you to either sit down or leave the plane. If you do not, I will call security to have you forcibly removed."

André glanced at the pilot and then back to Nicole. "Are you coming?"

Her heart told Nicole that's exactly what she wanted to do. But André, and the country, would pay the price of her lack of self-discipline, for sneaking into the big house on the hill and getting caught. She had no right to have and hold André and all he represented.

Struggling, she searched for the courage to say no. "I can't be the cause of you losing the election."

"Very well, Princess. If that is how it must be."

In a deceptively swift motion, he unbuckled her seat belt and lifted her over his shoulder.

"No! You can't do this to me again!" She flailed her fists against his back and kicked her feet in the air.

The woman across the aisle cheered, "Well done!" and neighboring passengers applauded.

"*Mademoiselle,* should I call security?" the pilot asked as André forced his way past him.

Nicole stifled a giggle. She didn't know if André's technique was romantic, but it certainly was persuasive. "No," she said with a resigned sigh. "He has a genetic tendency to kidnap women. I'm sure I can eventually cure him of the problem." Given fifty or sixty years.

If he was willing to go to so much trouble and risk the election, then how could she argue further? Not that he was prepared to give her much choice. Somehow, win or lose, together they'd find a way to help the country.

Once out of the plane, he was good enough to set her on her feet again, but never once did he allow her to catch her breath. They were out of the airport, into his car and racing through the main street of San Margo before she got out the words "Where are you taking me now?" The man was impossibly arrogant to think she'd go just anywhere he said without voicing some complaint. Wife or not, he couldn't boss her around that much.

"We are almost there."

"Where is *there?*" she asked in frustration.

He slid the Ferrari to a stop on the cobbled street in front of the cathedral steps. "Here. Where it all began."

Puzzled, she looked up at the soaring spires, so tall they reached right into the clouds. And beyond. In a glorious moment, the clouds parted, allowing a column of sunlight to burst through the opening. The sight took her breath away.

André's hand cupped her cheek and she looked into his dark, seductive eyes. "This time we are going to do it right."

"Do what?" she asked, still confused.

"Get married."

"I thought we'd already done that." Rather hurriedly, she admitted, but so far it had worked pretty well.

"This time we will marry in the cathedral. A woman should be able to live her dream."

"Now?" She frowned. "I'm hardly dressed for the occasion." A denim skirt and cotton blouse certainly didn't qualify as a wedding gown in her book. Nor did André's jeans quite hit the mark.

"Assuming Sebastian has followed my instructions, a suitable dress is waiting for you inside. The one you admired at the designer shop."

"Oh, André. That was so expensive." The train by itself must have required fifteen yards of the exquisite tulle.

"It is but a small trifling."

"Several thousand dollars' worth of trifles, I imagine."

He grinned at her, his easy way with money something she might never get used to. "Now, we have friends and family waiting to be our witnesses. *Grand-mère*. Sebastian. His parents, of course. Even Petra. And this time when you say 'I will,' I want to know that you love me as a wife should love a husband."

"Of course I love you." Emotion gathering in her chest, she caught his wrist in a tender grip. "And what of you, my dark, handsome prince. Do you love me?"

"I would think that has been most obvious for some time."

"Assume I'm new to the traditions of this country. I'd like to hear you say the words."

"Ah, my beautiful princess." He dipped his head and whispered in her ear all the words she had longed to hear. He told her how he would spend the rest of his life kneeling at her feet, that he would fill her life with the sweet smell of violets so she would never forget how much he loved her. When he ran out of words, he picked up the small bouquet of violets that had spilled onto the floorboard and placed it in her hands. "With these flowers," he said in a voice filled with emotion, "I pledge to you my love for as long as we both shall live."

She breathed deeply of the sweet scent, and tears of joy filled her eyes. No other ceremony would ever mean as much to her as his vow of love at this very moment. Nor would any words spoken by a priest bind her as tightly to her handsome prince.

BY THE NEXT MORNING news of André's determination to give up his chance of election for the love of his wife made headlines in every Margolis paper. The international press picked up the story, calling it a Cinderella fairy tale come true. There were even rumors of local telephone lines so jammed with people talking about André and his "princess" that business calls couldn't get through.

None of the attention, however, seemed to have made any difference in the early polls on election day. Hendrik and André, along with their respective supporters, were running neck and neck.

At the Labor party gathering in the ballroom of the San Margo Hotel, André kept Nicole close to his side. She felt as though he was afraid to let her out of his sight for fear she'd try to skip the country again. That definitely wasn't her plan. If nothing else had convinced her, the wedding night he'd planned certainly had. André had rented the entire *castle*, for heaven's sake, and they'd made love in the queen's bedchamber by the light of a hundred flickering candles. And the room, like the cathedral, had been filled to overflowing with violets.

Smiling at the memory, Nicole decided her own special prince had a romantic streak worthy of royal notice.

He'd also promised her she could create her own business here in Margolis, an antique searching service that would fill specific requests from clients in the States. It was an exciting opportunity that would assure Margolis families received top dollar for heirlooms they wanted to sell; a unique way for her to use her talents for the good of the people in her ancestral homeland.

Truth was, she had forced André to agree to that compromise about her working after she learned he had never arranged shipment to the States for the antiques she had already purchased. Boy, had she been miffed. But her anger hadn't lasted long. How could it when he'd kept kissing her senseless?

The roomful of Labor party officials hushed as the first election returns appeared on a huge overhead TV screen. She strained to interpret the results.

"Hendrik looks to be easily winning his district," André said next to her, his hand resting at her waist. "We expected that." He paused a moment, and she held her breath. "And I am well ahead in Montiard County."

"I should think so," she commented. "Everyone I met certainly loves you."

He gave her a little squeeze. "Our man in the north district is winning, but in the south it does not look so good. Here in central San Margo... That is peculiar.''

"What's wrong?"

"A monarchist candidate—Vilhelm Seville—is well ahead in his district.''

A buzz of conversation spread across the crowded room as everyone realized the minority party candidate was making a serious run for the central district seat. Meanwhile, Hendrik's and André's supporters seemed to be splitting the rest of the country right down the middle. Neither major party, it seemed, could claim a majority. Toward the end of the evening it became obvious that Seville and his monarchist followers would hold the balance of power in parliament.

"What will that mean?" Nicole asked.

André's dark brows lowered into a solid line. "I am not sure.''

At midnight, Seville appeared at the hotel ballroom with a small entourage of followers and requested a private meeting with André. Half an hour later, Nicole was called into the room.

André beamed her a smile. "Monsieur Seville and his people have agreed to support me as prime minister.''

Relieved and delighted beyond her wildest expectations, she raced across the room to shake the monarchist's hand. "I'm so glad, *monsieur*. I know you won't be sorry. André will do everything in his power—"

André halted her with his words. "They have one condition, however, before a final vote is cast in parliament."

She slanted André a glance. Since he was still smiling, she assumed the condition met with his approval. Though what kind of political agreement the two of them had concocted was beyond her imaginings.

"Since they have no legitimate heir to the throne whom they could support," André continued, his smile broadening as an amused twinkle appeared in his dark eyes, "they wish *you* to accept an honorary position . . . as the Queen of Margolis."

Her jaw slack, she stared at both men incredulously. "Me? Queen?"

"We would be honored if you would accept, *Madame*," Seville said. "You would be a symbol of all the good and beauty that is our country. You would give our children hope for the future, return to them a chance to dream again."

André slipped his arm possessively around her waist. "Of course, I will have the privilege of being the queen's consort."

Her heart filled with so much love and joy she could barely contain the emotion, Nicole looked up at her dark, handsome prince and knew dreams could come true. And if she had correctly interpreted the queasiness in her stomach that morning—and if Petra's prediction was accurate—she suspected the first of three dark-haired heirs to the House of Montiard was on the way.

HARLEQUIN®

A M E R I C A N ◆ R O M A N C E®

You asked for it...and now you've got it. More MEN!

We're thrilled to bring you another special edition of the popular
MORE THAN MEN series.

Like those who have come before him, Sean Seaward is more than tall,
dark and handsome. All of these men have extraordinary powers that
make them "more than men." But whether they are able to grant you
three wishes or to live forever, make no mistake—their greatest,
most extraordinary power is that of seduction.

So make a date next month with Sean Seaward in
#538 KISSED BY THE SEA
by Rebecca Flanders

SUPH5

Take 4 bestselling love stories FREE

Plus get a FREE surprise gift!

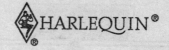

EXPECTATIONS
Shannon Waverly

Eternity, Massachusetts, is a town with something special going for it. According to legend, those who marry in Eternity's chapel are destined for a lifetime of happiness. As long as the legend holds true, couples will continue to flock here to marry and local businesses will thrive.

Unfortunately for the town, Marion and Geoffrey Kent are about to prove the legend wrong!

EXPECTATIONS, available in July from Harlequin Romance®, is the second book in Harlequin's new cross-line series, **WEDDINGS, INC.** Be sure to look for the third book, **WEDDING SONG,** by
Vicki Lewis Thompson (Harlequin Temptation® #502), coming in August.

WED-2

American Romance is goin' to the chapel…with three soon–to–be–wed couples. Only thing is, saying "I do" is the farthest thing from their minds!

You're cordially invited to join us for three months of veils and vows. Don't miss any of the nuptials in

May 1994	#533	THE EIGHT-SECOND WEDDING by Anne McAllister
June 1994	#537	THE KIDNAPPED BRIDE by Charlotte Maclay
July 1994	#541	VEGAS VOWS by Linda Randall Wisdom

GTC

A NEW STAR COMES OUT TO SHINE....

American Romance continues to search the heavens for the best new talent... the best new stories.

Join us next month when a new star appears in the American Romance constellation:

Rosemary Grace
#544 HONKY TONK DREAMS
July 1994

Sam Triver had heard of unusual ways to meet a woman, but never this unusual. When he walked into the newsroom, there stood transplanted Texan Lonnie "Lone Star" Stockton—her six-guns pointed to the ceiling. It may not have been love at first sight—but you couldn't deny that sparks were flying!

Be sure to Catch a "Rising Star"!

RISING STAR

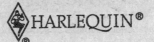

HARLEQUIN®

Don't miss these Harlequin favorites by some of our most distinguished authors!
And now, you can receive a discount by ordering two or more titles!

HT #25551	THE OTHER WOMAN by Candace Schuler	$2.99	☐
HT #25539	FOOLS RUSH IN by Vicki Lewis Thompson	$2.99	☐
HP #11550	THE GOLDEN GREEK by Sally Wentworth	$2.89	☐
HP #11603	PAST ALL REASON by Kay Thorpe	$2.99	☐
HR #03228	MEANT FOR EACH OTHER by Rebecca Winters	$2.89	☐
HR #03268	THE BAD PENNY by Susan Fox	$2.99	☐
HS #70532	TOUCH THE DAWN by Karen Young	$3.39	☐
HS #70540	FOR THE LOVE OF IVY by Barbara Kaye	$3.39	☐
HI #22177	MINDGAME by Laura Pender	$2.79	☐
HI #22214	TO DIE FOR by M.J. Rodgers	$2.89	☐
HAR #16421	HAPPY NEW YEAR, DARLING by Margaret St. George	$3.29	☐
HAR #16507	THE UNEXPECTED GROOM by Muriel Jensen	$3.50	☐
HH #28774	SPINDRIFT by Miranda Jarrett	$3.99	☐
HH #28782	SWEET SENSATIONS by Julie Tetel	$3.99	☐

Harlequin Promotional Titles

#83259	UNTAMED MAVERICK HEARTS	$4.99	☐

(Short-story collection featuring Heather Graham Pozzessere, Patricia Potter, Joan Johnston)
(limited quantities available on certain titles)

DEDUCT:	**AMOUNT**	$
	10% DISCOUNT FOR 2+ BOOKS	$
	POSTAGE & HANDLING	$
	($1.00 for one book, 50¢ for each additional)	
	APPLICABLE TAXES*	$ _____
	TOTAL PAYABLE	$ _____
	(check or money order—please do not send cash)	

To order, complete this form and send it, along with a check or money order for the total above, payable to Harlequin Books, to: **In the U.S.:** 3010 Walden Avenue, P.O. Box 9047, Buffalo, NY 14269-9047; **In Canada:** P.O. Box 613, Fort Erie, Ontario, L2A 5X3.

Name: _____

Address: _____ City: _____

State/Prov.: _____ Zip/Postal Code: _____

*New York residents remit applicable sales taxes.
Canadian residents remit applicable GST and provincial taxes.

HBACK-AJ